DOG WHISPERER

THE
GHOST

By Nicholas Edwards

SCHOLASTIC INC.

ISBN 978-0-545-56253-9

12 11 10 9 8 7 6 5 4 3 2 1   13 14 15 16 17 18/0

Printed in the U.S.A.   40

First Scholastic printing, January 2013

Design by Barbara Grzeslo

1

Emily was having a very strange birthday. *Any* birthday which happened in the middle of a hurricane was definitely going to be weird, but so far, hers had been totally and completely—well—*weird*. Peculiar. Odd. Different. Confusing. Eventful. *Exhausting.*

One thing for sure, she was never going to forget turning twelve!

Now, she was in her parents' car, and they were riding home—and she mostly just wanted to take a nap.

"Quite a day," her father said, from the front passenger's seat.

Emily had to wake herself up to nod. "Yeah, it sure was," she said, and gave her dog, Zachary—although she also called him Zack—a pat on the head. He must have been worn out, too, because all he did was wag his tail twice, without opening his eyes. Her cat, Josephine, was sound asleep in her carrier, and even snoring a little.

"Well, we'll be home soon," her mother said, slowing down for a stop sign. Normally, they would have just gone right down the dirt road to their house, but so many trees had crashed down all over Bailey's Cove, that they had to take the long way around. "But, this birthday is certainly going to be one to remember!"

Emily nodded again. *That* was an understatement.

The day had started inside her town's emergency shelter, where she and her parents—and, of course, Zachary and Josephine—had been evacuated to escape the storm. So, that alone would have made it an unusual day.

But then, with Zack's help, she had spent the morning rescuing her very mean neighbor, Mrs. Griswold, from the wreckage of what had once been a nice living room. After that, she had been down at the boatyard all afternoon, trying to help her best friend Bobby rebuild his boat. She and Bobby had been working on the boat for *weeks*—and the hurricane had destroyed it in a matter of *seconds*. It would have been a beautiful wooden dinghy, but now, it was just a pile of splintered wood.

All of that would have been enough to make her birthday feel very complicated, but the worst part was something Mrs. Griswold had told her by accident. Her neighbor had been pinned under part of her roof, and a fallen tree. While they were waiting for the ambulance, they had had an awkward conversation to pass the time.

And, out of nowhere, Mrs. Griswold had said something bad about Emily's parents.

Well, not *bad*, exactly, but upsetting. Emily had always known that she had been adopted right after she was born. Of course, since she was biracial, and her parents were Caucasian, she probably would have figured it out on her own, anyway. She had never been told anything about either of her birth parents, and she was pretty sure that her parents didn't know anything about them, either, because they had never been able to answer any of her questions.

Except that Mrs. Griswold said that her parents had *known* her birth mother, like maybe she had been a friend of theirs, or something.

So now, Emily couldn't help wondering whether her parents just hadn't *wanted* to answer her questions.

If, of course, what Mrs. Griswold had said was even true.

Which she was pretty sure that it wasn't, because her parents would never do that to her.

Would they?

She hoped not, anyway. Besides, Mrs. Griswold was famous for being scary and cranky and unfriendly, so she had probably just been making a bad joke or something.

Emily had been waiting all afternoon to ask her parents about it, but it had never seemed like the right time. A lot of the lobster boats and sailboats down at the marina had been badly damaged by the storm, and they had all been too busy trying to help people clean up to have a conversation.

When everyone took a break at one point, her mother had somehow managed to scare up a few dozen cupcakes and some soda. So, they all stopped for a snack, and everyone sang "Happy Birthday" to her, which was really nice. It was also pretty funny, because some of the fishermen and dock workers were *completely* off-key.

They had turned onto their dirt road now, and Emily could tell that her parents were very tense. None of them had seen the house yet, so they had no idea how much damage to expect.

"Well, if it's gone," her father said heartily, "we'll just start driving south until we find a good hotel somewhere."

Her mother laughed nervously. "Yes, that sounds like a good plan. Then, we'll stake out a plot of land, and start fresh."

Her father nodded. "Build a cabin with our own little hands."

The house couldn't actually be *gone*, right? That would be too awful. They hadn't heard any news about how bad—or not—the storm had been in the rest of Maine. But, their part of the state, on the coastline, had been hit really hard.

Once they turned onto their street, her mother drove very cautiously. There were so many branches on the road that they had to stop twice, and Emily and her mother would have to get out of the car to move them out of the way. Her father couldn't help much, because he had broken his ankle during the storm, and was going to be on crutches for the next six weeks or so. Zachary barked each time they stopped, and Emily knew he wanted to help, but she thought it would be safer for him to stay in the car.

Then, finally, they saw their house—and her parents both let out huge sighs of relief. It was obvious that there had been a big storm, but mostly, it looked okay. A few of the shutters had blown off, and at least two of the upstairs windows were smashed, including one in her bedroom. The backyard was covered with broken branches and torn-off leaves, but as far as Emily could tell, they had been lucky enough not to lose any trees. A massive branch had landed on top of their garage, and part of the roof had been crushed, but it was still intact, otherwise. And their picnic table had blown over, and ended up about twenty feet away from their wooden deck.

Her father let out his breath. "Well, okay. It looks as though we were pretty lucky."

Her mother nodded. "Thank goodness. I was really expecting us to come back to a disaster area."

The path of the storm's destruction had been pretty random. Down at the boatyard, some of the boats were completely untouched, while the boats on either side had been destroyed. The same thing seemed to be true, as far as the houses and other buildings in town were concerned—some were fine, and some had been severely damaged. It didn't make much sense, but Emily figured she should probably just be grateful that their house seemed to be okay.

They went inside, first, to get Josephine settled down and to see how much broken glass needed to be cleaned up, and whether there had been any water damage. Emily's bedroom had so much glass on the floor that she had to grab Zack's collar to keep him from bounding into the room and maybe getting cut by accident. He was a big white retriever mix who weighed just over a hundred pounds, so she had to hang on with both hands to keep him safe.

"Stay!" Emily said. "Good boy."

Zack wagged his tail, and peered curiously into the room.

One of the windows had blown in completely, but

the other one was just cracked. It looked as though the pounding rain had reached all the way over by her desk.

"Do you think my computer's all right?" Emily asked her father, who was just coming up the stairs, very slow on his crutches.

He nodded. "It should be, but I don't want you to go in there until your mother and I take care of the glass. Why don't you take Josephine down to the guest room, and get her all set up, so she won't start wandering around in all of this mess? You and she and Zack can bunk in there tonight, and we'll try to get someone in to fix the windows first thing tomorrow."

Emily nodded, since that sounded like a good idea.

Josephine was complaining bitterly inside her carrier, yowling loudly, although she was also lying on her back, playing with a little catnip ball, so she seemed to be happy enough.

"Come on, Zack," Emily said, and led him down the hall with one hand hooked through his collar, while she lugged Josephine's carrier in the other hand.

Once they were in the guest room, Emily carefully closed the door, so that neither of her pets would be in danger of cutting their paws anywhere else in the house. She opened the carrier door, and Josephine stalked out. She was a very small tiger cat, but she had a *big*—and fierce—personality. She hissed loudly at Zachary—who was just standing in the middle of the rug, not doing a single thing in the world to bother anyone. Zachary let out a sad, soft whine in response, because he was a very sensitive dog, and his feelings got easily hurt.

Emily quickly fixed Josephine up with her litter box, some fresh water—from one of the many bottles her parents had bought before the storm—and a dish of cat food. It was only about six thirty, which meant that it would still be light outside for about another hour. So, Emily went downstairs to help her father check the yard again to make sure that everything was okay, while Zack galloped around the wet grass and tangled piles of branches, barking happily. Emily's mother was still inside, covering the broken windows with thick sheets of plastic, and sweeping up all of the glass.

It was pretty windy outside, and the air smelled even more briny and salty than usual. Their house was right on the water, and the ocean was grey and choppy, with waves slapping against the rocky shore.

"I guess we should pile up most of the branches over here," her father said, using one of his crutches to point towards the stack over by the garage. "When everything dries out a little, we can put it all on the kindling pile."

Emily nodded. Every fall, her parents bought a cord or two of firewood from Mr. and Mrs. Bolduc, who ran a

Christmas tree farm on the outskirts of town. But, during the year, she and her parents would pile smaller branches and sticks into a big, neat stack, and use the kindling all winter long to help start fires in their fireplaces.

She was pretty sure that Zachary was going to *love* lying in front of cozy fires at night. She had found him during the summer, after he had almost drowned and washed up on the rocks by their house. So, even though it seemed as though he had *always* been part of her life, this would actually be his first winter with them.

"Can you do it, though, on your crutches?" Emily asked.

Her father looked down at his cast, which was already a little muddy, and sighed. "No. Probably not."

"Well, I can get started," Emily said.

Her father nodded. "Okay, just for a few minutes, though. Not much fun to spend your birthday doing a bunch of work."

Zachary seemed to think that the sticks and branches were all part of a special game, because every time Emily put a branch down on the pile, he would grab the other end and try to get her to play fetch.

When Zack pulled the pile apart for the fourth time, her father laughed.

"Okay, let's call it a day," he said. "Why don't we go

over to the Peabodys' house, and make sure everything is all right over there, before we head in?"

Their neighbors, the Peabodys, were down in Florida—they were retired now, and spent at least half of the year there—so they had missed the storm entirely. But, a couple of days earlier, Emily's father and one of their other neighbors, Dr. Henrik, had gone over and closed all of the shutters, and put tape on the windows, and moved the lawn furniture into the garage, and that sort of thing.

Emily and her father walked—well, her father *limped*—around the Peabodys' house, while Zachary wandered along behind them, wagging his tail and playing with sticks.

"Does it hurt?" Emily asked.

Her father shook his head. "No, it's not so bad. I guess it's a little uncomfortable, maybe."

It probably *did* hurt a lot, since she had seen him wince a few times, but he was moving along pretty well, at least.

For the most part, everything at their neighbors' house looked okay, but they found a wheelbarrow that had blown up onto the porch, and the mailbox was just plain *gone*. Then, as they rounded the corner of the house, they saw that a bunch of tree limbs had fallen onto the Peabodys' garden, and crushed a lot of the plants.

Above them, some of the trees were creaking loudly as they swayed in the wind, and her father glanced up.

"I think we'll have to see how soon we can get a tree surgeon to come out here and take a look," he said.

Emily laughed. "They're actually called *surgeons*? Do they have to go to special schools and everything?"

Her father thought about that. "I assume so. But, I don't actually know," he said, and took out his iPhone so that he could look it up on the Internet. "Oh. Right," he said, and then sighed and put it away, since no one in town had had any cell phone service for *hours* now.

"It's totally weird not to be able to get on the Internet," Emily said.

Her father nodded. "I hope we get our service back soon, because I am *definitely* going through withdrawal."

Emily was, too, actually, especially because she hadn't been able to check her email for—wow, more than a whole day now! She started to say something, but then stopped, sensing that her dog was alarmed a split second *before* she saw him straighten up, looking very alert. She wasn't sure what was bothering him, until she heard the creaking sounds above them turn into a loud *cracking* sound.

A massive tree limb had just broken off—and it was going to hit her father!

"Dad, look out!" Emily yelled.

Her father glanced around in confusion, just as Zachary slammed into him at top speed and knocked him off his feet and into a pile of wet leaves. Before her father could even open his mouth to protest, there was a loud whooshing noise, and then, a *huge* branch crashed onto the ground right where her father had been standing a few seconds earlier. The branch was so big and heavy that the ground actually *shook* when it landed.

"Wow," her father said, and blinked. "That was—wow."

"Are you okay?" Emily asked nervously.

Her father nodded, picking himself up and brushing off wet leaves. "I'm fine. It didn't get anywhere near *you*, did it?"

Emily shook her head. "No, I'm okay."

"Good," her father said. "Let's hope I didn't break the *other* ankle."

Emily stared at him.

He grinned at her. "Sorry, bad joke."

Whew. Emily gathered up his crutches, and used her sleeve to wipe off the wet leaves and dirt from them.

Before taking his crutches from her, her father reached over to pat Zachary on the head. "What a good dog you are. Thank you!"

Zack wagged his tail, and then held up his right paw.

"Um, does he want me to shake it?" her father asked uncertainly. He had never had a dog before in his whole life, so a lot of the things Zachary did still pretty much *baffled* him.

Emily shook her head again. "No, he got a lot of mud stuck in his paw, and he really hates that." She bent down and carefully cleaned away the mud from between each toe, and off his claws, and Zack wagged his tail in response.

"There are times when I really think you two read each other's minds," her father said.

The honest truth—and the most complicated part of her life these days—was that she *could* read Zachary's mind, sort of.

Sort of exactly.

She didn't understand it, but ever since the night she had found him, the two of them had been connected, somehow. When he was hungry, she felt hungry. When he was sleepy, she started yawning.

And when someone—*anyone*—was in trouble, she would find herself helping them somehow.

It was completely cool, and had totally changed her life, but sometimes, the whole thing seemed overwhelming, too. She hadn't been able to figure out a good way to tell her parents yet, so the only people who knew about it were her best friends, Bobby and Karen.

"Is his paw okay now?" her father asked.

Emily realized that she was still holding Zack's right paw, and she carefully lowered it to the ground. "Yeah, he's fine now," she said, although she checked his left front paw, too, just to be sure.

"Well, let's go get him a special reward treat of some kind," her father said, maneuvering his crutches so that he could stand up again.

Emily instinctively pictured a box of dog biscuits, and Zack must have been paying close attention, because he barked a happy bark. She didn't understand why the two of them could send each other images, and instantly understand them—but, they could, and they *did*, constantly.

When they got inside, her mother was impressed, and distressed, when she heard about the tree limb that had fallen. She patted Zachary on the head and gave him two biscuits, which he carried over to the rug near the kitchen door. Then, he flopped down to eat them, chewing noisily.

Apparently, the telephone and electrical wires were down all over Bailey's Cove, and it looked as though they weren't going to get their power back anytime soon. But, they had plenty of flashlights and some battery-powered lanterns for light, and if they needed more, they had a bunch of candles, too. The water was still running, but the town was advising that people either not drink it, or boil it for a few minutes, first. Luckily, her parents had bought a lot of bottled water before the storm hit, and they had filled up a bunch of plastic containers with tap water, too. Both bathtubs were also full, and Emily assumed that was water they could use for washing, since the idea of *drinking* it wasn't really all that appealing.

With the power off, her parents were afraid that all of the food in the refrigerator and freezer was going to spoil. As a result, they had decided to finish off as much as they could, and throw away the rest. If the power came back in the next twelve hours or so, they could probably save some of the stuff in the freezer, but judging from the amount of damage to the telephone and electrical poles outside, that didn't seem likely. Besides, her birthday cake was tucked away inside the freezer, and she would have been kind of disappointed if they didn't get to eat it on her actual birthday.

So, they had an unusual supper of bottled water, sliced tomatoes, carrot sticks, bananas, cheese, crackers, peanut butter, and rye bread. Emily had been a vegetarian for about three years now, so that was all fine with her. But, her father didn't look particularly excited about his dinner, and she had a feeling that he might open a can of ravioli or chili or something later and eat it cold.

"Not exactly the birthday supper we had in mind," her mother said, serving each of them some yoghurt with cut-up fruit mixed in.

No, they had been planning to create a big feast of homemade Mexican food. They were even going to make a couple of different kinds of fresh salsa, and everything.

"It still all tastes good," Emily said.

"We can make up for it, as soon as the power is back," her father promised. "And we'll drive into Brunswick or down to Portland or someplace tomorrow, and find a nice fancy dinner somewhere."

"And we can still cook Mexican food soon, right?" Emily asked. She'd been particularly looking forward to the part where they were going to roast chipotle peppers, and grind their own cumin, and all.

"Absolutely," her mother said. "Maybe that's what we can do when your grandparents get here."

Since the local airports had closed because of the hurricane, her grandparents had to postpone their trip. Originally, they had been planning to be there on her birthday, but now, they were hoping to come up next weekend, instead.

Emily nodded enthusiastically. Her grandparents on her father's side lived in New York, and usually liked to order in food every night, instead of cooking on their own. But, she knew they would be happy to make an exception in this case.

When they were finished with their supper-that-felt-more-like-an-afternoon-snack, Emily went into the den, so that her parents could get the cake ready without her watching. When they called her back in, there was a chocolate cake with chocolate-chip ice cream filling and frozen mocha whipped cream for frosting, waiting for her on the kitchen table. Her name was spelled across the top in brightly colored M&M's, too.

Her parents sang "Happy Birthday" to her, and then, Emily blew out the candles with one burst of air—twelve blue candles, with one to grow on.

"Happy birthday!" her mother said. "Do you feel any different now?"

"*Very* old," Emily said. "And mature."

Her father nodded. "You look so mature, that I might not even have recognized you."

Since the cake wasn't going to last very long with the freezer off, they could eat as much as they wanted, which was fun. It was melting pretty quickly, but still tasted great.

Josephine jumped onto the table and tasted the whipped cream on the cake—which made Emily's father cringe a little. He did his best to be comfortable around their pets, but for him, it was still a very long work-in-progress.

"Don't worry, we'll cut off that part, Theo," Emily's mother said.

He nodded emphatically. "We'd better, yeah. To be safe."

Emily never worried much about cat *or* dog germs, but it would make her father shudder if she reminded him of that.

Before the storm hit, they had bought a special battery-operated emergency radio, which was designed to pick up weather reports. But, they also had an old AM/FM radio that also used batteries, and after supper, they went into the den to listen to the Red Sox game.

It was dark out now, but her mother had set up two of their lanterns, too, and the den felt nice and cozy. So, they played Monopoly for a while, and they also had their e-book readers.

Of course, they could read *actual* books, if they wanted, but the light was pretty dim.

They listened to the baseball game, until it was over, and the Red Sox had, unfortunately, lost *again*.

It was very quiet in the room. Josephine was on Emily's lap, purring, and Zack had climbed up onto the couch next to her. Her father was in an easy chair across from her, with his ankle propped up on some pillows on the coffee table, and her mother was in the antique rocking chair.

"It's been an awfully long day," her mother said. "I think it's really time for all of us to get some sleep."

It *had* been a long day, and none of them had gotten much sleep the night before, inside the hurricane shelter.

Still, this seemed like it might be a good time to talk to her parents, while it was so quiet and there were no distractions. They couldn't turn on the television, none of the phones were going to ring, and their computers weren't working, so there weren't going to be any outside interruptions.

The mood in the room was nice and relaxed, and Emily didn't want to change that. But, she had a huge question she wanted—and needed—to ask. A question she had been *waiting* to ask for hours. She was afraid to bring it up, though. She patted Zack, trying to make up her mind.

"What?" her father said. "You look very worried."

"Is it okay if I ask an important question?" Emily asked. "I don't want you guys to be upset."

Her parents both shrugged.

"Sure," her mother said. "Why not?"

Okay. After all, her parents always said that she could talk to them about *anything*, so maybe they wouldn't mind her bringing this up? Emily took a deep breath. "Did both of you know my mother? Like, as a friend, not a stranger? My birth mother, I mean?"

For a minute, it was completely silent in the room, and then her parents exchanged uneasy glances.

Wait, did that mean that it was *true*? Emily stared at them.

"Who told you that?" her father asked.

Did it matter? And wasn't the important part that her parents, who *should* have told her, didn't? "I know it's true," Emily said, "and I feel like you guys should, you know, tell me about it."

It was very quiet again.

Her father sighed. "We don't know very much, Emily. We really don't."

"But, you know a lot more about it than I thought," Emily said.

Her parents exchanged glances again, and then nodded.

"So, can you tell me about her?" Emily asked.

Her mother let out her breath. "I guess this conversation is long overdue, but—well, it's complicated. Are you sure you want to get into it tonight? Maybe we could wait until tomorrow morning, or—"

The longer they waited, the more tense they were all going to be. Emily shook her head. "I'd really rather do it tonight. I mean, I know you guys are tired and everything, but—" She was feeling guilty now, so she decided to stop and just concentrate on patting Zachary.

"I think this is a good time to talk about it," her father said. "We've probably put it off for too long, but we wanted to wait until you were a little older. But, twelve is probably a good age for it."

Her mother nodded. "Your father's right. This is probably as good a time as we're likely to find, and—" She sighed. "Okay. Sure. Let's talk about it."

Emily wasn't sure if she was excited—or scared, but for the first time in her life, she was actually going to learn a lot more about who she was, and where she had come from.

Wow!

Of course, now that they had decided to talk about it, there was nothing but awkward silence in the room. In fact, when Josephine yawned and stretched, Emily and her parents all jumped.

"So, you knew my mother?" Emily asked. She had almost said "my real mother," but managed to catch herself at the last second. "My birth mother, I mean?"

Her parents looked at each other for a long minute.

"We didn't *know* her, exactly," her mother said, after a pause. "But, yes, we did, in a manner of speaking."

That was such an incredibly vague answer that Emily frowned.

"We had wanted a child ever since we got married," her father said. "And we had registered with adoption agencies, and—well, so much time went by. After a while, I don't think either of us really believed that it would ever happen."

None of that was new information, but Emily nodded

receptively. It made sense that her parents might want to ease into the whole subject.

There was another silence in the room, which seemed to stretch out for a really long time.

Finally, her mother broke it. "She was a student at the college. I hadn't had her in class, and neither had your father, but she confided in—" She stopped. "A colleague," she said finally.

Okay, that meant that the "colleague" was someone Emily knew, probably a professor friend of her parents.

"She didn't know what she was going to do," her mother went on. "But, she didn't think she was ready to raise a child, and—well, she was leaning very strongly towards a completely closed adoption. But then, she decided that she would rather *know* something about who her child's parents were going to be. And, in the end, she was generous and loving enough to be willing to allow us to have the great honor of being your parents."

That made it all *sound* really noble on her birth mother's part, and maybe it was—but, it certainly didn't *feel* that way.

"And then, just, what," Emily said. "Back to her normal life, like nothing ever happened?"

She must have sounded very tense, and maybe even angry, because Zachary made an anxious little whining sound, and she quickly patted him a few times, so that he wouldn't worry.

Her father shook his head. "No, of course not. It had to have been a completely life-changing event for her. She withdrew from the college while she was pregnant, and ultimately ended up transferring someplace else. But, when she went into labor, we flew down right away, so that we could be at the hospital during the birth. I'm sorry, I meant, during *your* birth," he corrected himself. "And then, a few days later, we brought you home."

That was all still a lot more vague than Emily wanted it to be. In fact, other than finding out that her birth mother had been a student, it wasn't anything she didn't already know. Except, wait, maybe there was another possible detail buried in there. "Flew down *where*?" she asked.

Her parents glanced at each other.

"Atlanta," her father said.

Okay. That was something specific. "So, I'm South-ern?" Emily said.

Her mother nodded. "Technically, yes, I guess you are, although I never really thought about it that way."

So, she was *from* somewhere. From a specific place. A *real* place, not something she had to imagine. There were so many different questions to ask that she really didn't know where to start. So, maybe she should just go with a really obvious question. "Was she African-American?" Emily asked.

Her parents nodded.

Okay. "Do I get to know her name?" Emily asked.

Her parents instantly shook their heads.

"I'm sorry," her mother said. "But, we *promised*. So, we could never do that without her permission. It would be a violation of the agreement."

Maybe, but who would know the difference? And she should certainly be allowed to know her own mother's name, shouldn't she? Emily frowned. "Are you guys in touch with her?"

Her mother didn't quite meet her eyes—which was very, very suspicious. "Once in a while," she said finally. "I send her occasional photos and notes."

"Does she answer them?" Emily asked.

Her mother shook her head. "Almost never."

Great. That was just great. Her birth mother wasn't even interested in finding out about her. She didn't realize she had clenched her fist until she felt Zack nuzzling her hand. So, with an effort, she loosened her fingers and patted him some more, instead. "Do you think she even looks at the pictures?" Emily asked.

Her mother nodded. "I'm quite sure she does. And once every year or two, she'll send an email and say thank you."

That didn't mean that Emily was about to nominate her to be Mother of the Year, though, did it?

"I know this is really hard for *you*, Emily," her father said, "but I think it's also very difficult for her. She had to make some really grueling decisions, and—well, your mother and I will never stop being grateful to her."

"Is she still in Atlanta?" Emily asked.

Right away, her parents shook their heads.

If they were that sure, then, they knew exactly where she *did* live—but, they probably weren't going to give her the details. "Do you know where she lives?" she asked.

"Somewhere near Washington, D.C.," her mother said. "Although I think she moved a couple of years ago, and I don't have that address."

This was so totally weird, and upsetting. "But, you know how to get in touch," Emily said.

Her mother nodded uneasily. "Yes."

Emily waited for her to give more details, and then realized that it wasn't going to happen.

"I don't think very many people in her life know about what happened," her father said, "and it's always been my sense that she wants to keep it that way."

Emily nodded stiffly. "Because she's ashamed."

"Not ashamed of *you*," her mother said quickly. "But, I know she must have a lot of regrets about not being able to keep you in her life, and I think she just decided to keep all of it in the past."

Maybe another clue was buried in there, too. "Are you saying that she's married now?" Emily asked.

Her mother nodded reluctantly.

Being married wasn't that big a deal, so there must be more to it, based upon her mother's uncomfortable expression. "Does she have children?" Emily asked.

Her mother sighed.

Oh, wow. That just couldn't be possible. Emily almost gasped. "You mean, children she *kept*?"

"Yes," her mother said. "She has twins. I think they would be about a year old now, although I'm not completely sure."

So, she did have children—and children she *wanted*. Children she was proud of, and loved, and didn't keep hidden. "You mean, children she liked better than me," Emily said.

"No, it's not that simple, Emily," her father said. "She's in a very different stage of her life now. She's in a situation where she's able to take care of them, which she wasn't, when she was a student."

All of this was really more than she felt as though she could take in, and she was suddenly feeling *unbelievably* tired, but Emily couldn't bring herself to stop asking questions, either. "So, she has like, this nice little family now," Emily said, "and I'm this big bad secret?"

Her mother sighed. "People do the best they can, Emily."

Maybe, but her birth mother's "best" seemed to be pretty lousy. "Do you think she would ever want to meet me?" Emily asked.

"I'm sure that, somewhere deep inside, she would want to get a chance to see you," her mother said, and then shook her head reluctantly. "But, I honestly don't think that's something she wants to have happen."

Oh. Emily tried not to look as crushed as she felt. "Can you ask her? The next time you get in touch with her?"

"Of course," her mother said. "I can't promise that she'll answer me, but I absolutely will ask. That's a promise from me."

Okay. And her mother—who was her *real* mother—always kept her promises.

"What matters the most, Emily, is that *we* get to have you as *our* child," her father said. "That's what's important to your mother and me."

Yeah. But, this was still all really upsetting. So, she might as well go for broke and ask the other important question. "What about my father?" Emily asked.

"She never told us," her mother answered. "In fact, I'm not sure she told *anyone*, even him."

What kind of person could walk around keeping total secrets like that? *Huge*, important secrets? Did Emily even want to be related to someone who could do that? Not that she had a choice, of course. "Was he a student, too?" she asked.

Her father shrugged. "Probably, but we just don't know."

"Do you even know if he was white or black?" Emily asked.

Her parents shook their heads.

It could be either, since she was reasonably light-skinned. Now that she was thinking about it, it was kind of weird that she didn't really wonder very much about her birth father. It was always the idea of her birth *mother* that loomed in her mind. But, the truth was that half of her came from someone who was obviously a complete stranger, even to her parents.

Emily slouched back against the couch cushions, rubbing her hands across her eyes for a few seconds. It wasn't that she felt like crying, exactly, but she felt— jumbled inside. And really, really confused. "When you send her photos and all, does she ask a bunch of questions?" she asked.

"She usually just thanks me, and doesn't say anything more than that," her mother said. "But, she was impressed by your sketch for the Faculty Contest."

Which had been of the lighthouse down on the point, on a windy day, with rocks and waves and seagulls everywhere. She had won second prize—and still, privately, thought that the first-prize winner, a splotchy oddly-colored mass of flowers and leaves, hadn't been nearly as good.

"You got robbed," her father said. "Those flowers were very mediocre."

Emily grinned in spite of herself, but decided not to admit that she agreed one hundred percent.

Two hundred percent.

"The fix was in that day, Little Emily," her father went on.

Emily wouldn't have thought that it was possible to break the tension in the room—but, that actually worked pretty well.

"You set a very poor example, Theo," her mother said, but she was smiling, too, now.

"Shenanigans!" her father said emphatically. "I tell you, there were shenanigans in that judging room!"

He probably really believed that, but Emily assumed that he was trying to change the subject, too. Whenever an umpire's call went against the Red Sox, her father was prone to shouting "I sense shenanigans!" at the television set. Once, when they had been at Fenway Park, he had yelled that at the field, but everyone sitting near them had stared at him. It had been funny, but also embarrassing.

"Do you have more questions?" her mother said.

Of course she did. But, they probably weren't questions that had any answers. "Yeah," Emily said. "But—I don't know. Maybe not any more today. I'm really tired."

Her parents nodded, both of them looking visibly relieved to hear that.

It was quiet again.

"I'm really sorry about all of this," her mother said. "Nothing that has been happening today is *remotely* the way I expected us to spend your birthday."

Yeah, it had been kind of a downer, all the way around, from start to finish. "I think I want to go to bed, but can we maybe eat the rest of the melted cake first?" Emily said.

Her father nodded enthusiastically. "We sure can!" he said.

So, they all went into the kitchen and ate the rest of the cake—which was delicious. They didn't talk about anything serious, either, which was nice. When they finished, her mother took Zachary out to the yard for a few minutes, while Emily carried Josephine upstairs to the guest room. Her father set up one of the battery-powered lanterns on the bedside table, but it still felt dark and shadowy in the room.

"Are you going to be okay?" he asked.

Emily nodded. "Yeah. But, I'll be glad when we get the power back."

"Maybe tomorrow, if we're lucky," he said.

She sure hoped so.

When she was ready for bed, her parents hugged her good night and tucked her in—and wished her happy birthday one last time.

"You're sure you're going to be able to sleep?" her mother asked. "Or do you want to talk some more?"

Emily *wasn't* sure about either of those things, but

she shook her head. "It's pretty late. I think I just want to crash."

After her parents left the room, Emily yawned—and laughed when Zachary yawned, too. Normally, she liked to read for a while before trying to go to sleep, but tonight she was too tired. It was nicer just to lie under the covers, and let her mind wander.

Even though it wanted to wander straight to *Atlanta*.

But, she should probably save that for another day. She was way too exhausted to think about all of this stuff tonight.

She wasn't afraid of the dark—exactly—but, Emily was glad that both Zack and Josephine were up on the bed with her, snuggling close. She didn't believe in monsters or ghosts or anything like that—well, not *much*— but, at least, if one showed up during the night, she wouldn't be outnumbered.

She thought she would be awake for hours, but the next thing she knew, it was morning, and the sun was coming in through her windows. Well, through the guest room windows, anyway.

It was Sunday, so they drove into Brunswick to go to church, where her mother sang in the choir every week. Some of the places in Brunswick had already gotten their electric power back, so they had a nice hot brunch at a local diner. Then, when they got home, they spent the rest of the day cleaning up the backyard, and helping their neighbors, the Henriks, clean up the Peabodys' yard, too. Emily's father was frustrated that he couldn't do much on his crutches, so he ended up sitting by the kindling pile on a lawn chair, breaking all of the sticks into manageable sizes.

Cyril, who operated the town's Mini-Mart, had arranged for some people—mostly underemployed fishermen who worked part-time as carpenters or handymen—to go down to Mrs. Griswold's house and start repairing the storm damage there, too.

Emily had kind of been hoping that school would be cancelled for the next week, but by Monday morning, the power was back almost everywhere—except for their neighborhood, and a few other coastal areas—and things around town felt as though they were getting back to normal.

Sometimes, one of Emily's parents drove her to school, but usually, she waited for the bus in front of the Mini-Mart. The Mini-Mart was one of those funny, tiny stores which seemed to carry *everything*, no matter how obscure it was. Sometimes, people in town liked to go in with a "Stump Cyril" request, and ask if he had any imported green capers or elderberry jelly or hairnets—and the answer was always yes. One afternoon, Emily had even been able to buy a horse's rubber curry comb there to use to brush Zachary.

Emily really liked Cyril, who was a gruff and tough Vietnam veteran whose bark was much, much louder than his bite. Unfortunately, he didn't like her friend Bobby, who had shoplifted a piece of candy back when he was about four years old—and Cyril had never forgiven him.

But, since Bobby and his older siblings were the only other kids who lived on the peninsula, it was Bobby's bus stop, too. So, he would come and wait there, carefully *not* stepping on the store's property.

Usually, Emily got there first, but this morning, Bobby had beaten her. He was sitting down on a tree stump by the side of the road, reading a book on boat-building. Before they had started working on the boat, she had *never* seen Bobby reading, but now he did all the time. Mostly, he read books about building boats, but he had started reading novels about boats and sailors, too.

Emily waved at the little group of locals sitting at the picnic table outside Cyril's store—they gathered every day for coffee and snacks and long conversations—and then, she sat on an old log near the tree stump.

"What happened to *The Cay*?" she asked, since that was the book he had been reading when they were in the hurricane shelter.

"Finished it last night," Bobby said. "It was like, old-fashioned and everything, but pretty cool. I'm going to ask Mrs. Billingham if she can give me something that's like, more modern, though."

Emily nodded. Mrs. Billingham was one of the town librarians, and when Bobby had shuffled up to the front desk and mumbled that he was maybe, you know, sort of looking for a book he might possibly like to read, she had looked startled—and then, delighted, and brought him several.

Cyril came stomping out of the store with a steaming pot of fresh coffee and a platter of Danishes for the group of people gathered at the picnic table. Rumor had it that Cyril baked all of his own pastries every morning, but Emily found that really hard to imagine.

He smiled and waved at her. "Good morning, Emily!" Then, he frowned at Bobby. "Were you on weekend furlough from the juvenile detention hall?"

Bobby shook his head solemnly. "Work release, sir."

Cyril looked as though he wanted to smile, but he sniffed, instead. "Well—get a haircut."

Bobby's hair *was* pretty long these days, and he looked as though he had just left a beach somewhere and was wondering where his surfboard was.

"Would you like a Danish, Emily?" Cyril asked.

She nodded. "Yes, please. Could I have one for my prison friend, too?"

Cyril grumbled, but came across the parking lot to give each of them one.

By the time they had finished their pastries, the bus *still* hadn't shown up.

"We're going to be totally late," Bobby said. "You think we'll get in trouble?"

Emily shook her head. "Everyone else on the bus is going to be late, too."

"Oh." He thought about that. "Yeah, good point."

Since she hadn't been able to use her email or telephone for the past couple of days, she hadn't talked to him at all.

"I found out my mother was a college student my parents knew," she said.

That got Bobby's full attention. "Seriously?" he said. "Wow."

She told him the whole story, during which he mostly kept shaking his head and saying, "Wow."

"So," he said, when she was finished. "Is it good that you know about this stuff now—or bad?"

She shrugged, because the honest answer was that she had no idea.

The bus was finally heading towards them, and they got on, finding seats near the back. A lot of the other buses had been late, too, apparently, because so many roads were still blocked by fallen branches and other debris, and that had caused delays all over the place. So, their principal, Mrs. Wilkins, had canceled first period, and everyone was supposed to go to their homerooms, instead, until second period.

Even the people who lived pretty far from the coast were full of stories about the storm. It seemed that the wind and rain had done a lot of damage to trees and houses and other buildings, even if they were miles away from the actual ocean. At least one small river had flooded, and washed out a bridge, too.

The school itself had some broken and cracked windows, which were heavily taped up, or were being repaired even while they were all sitting in class.

The goalie nets on the soccer field had blown into the nearby woods, one of the poles holding up a net and backboard on the outdoor basketball court was completely tilted to one side, a tree had fallen on top of the backstop on the baseball field, and trash cans had been thrown all over the place. It was a mess, and she could see the custodians outside, trying to clean it up.

Her other best friend, Karen, was in her homeroom. Normally, they not only emailed each other and talked on the phone a lot, but they texted constantly, too. So, it had been strange to be out of contact all weekend. She had known Karen since they had taken a Tiny Tots swimming class at the college, when they were about three years old. Karen loved music more than anything else, and could play any instrument she picked up, although piano and saxophone were her favorites.

While they were waiting for second period to start, Emily told Karen about her latest news—and, like Bobby, Karen said, "Wow" several times, in response.

"How do you feel about it?" Karen asked, after hearing all of the details.

That was a good question—that still didn't have a definite answer. "I don't know," Emily said. "It feels like a big adjustment."

"But, you know *some* stuff now, at least," Karen said. "So, it's not just this total blank in your mind."

Yes, but it was both more—and *less*—than she wanted to know, in many ways. She now knew where she had been born, that her mother must be smart, since she got into a really demanding college, and that she was probably never going to have any idea who her birth father was, except that he maybe—possibly, perhaps—had gone to Bowdoin, too.

"It doesn't seem right that she has *twins* now," Emily said, "but doesn't bother getting in touch with me."

"Maybe she feels like she would be getting in your way," Karen guessed.

Maybe. But, as far as Emily was concerned, it just seemed cowardly.

"If you'd grown up in Atlanta, you probably would have had a Southern accent and all," Karen said.

That was true. Emily considered that. "You're right. I would be completely different, wouldn't I?"

Karen nodded. "Yeah, you'd be saying 'Y'all,' and calling people 'sugar' and 'honey' and things like that."

Which was hard to imagine. Her actual accent was a combination of New York and California, with New England expressions like "wicked" creeping in here and there. "Do you think I would still be myself?" Emily asked curiously.

Karen looked very wise. "Nature or nurture. Hmmm."

She sounded so serious, that Emily laughed. "Tell me what you think, Professor Mankins." Karen's father, Dr. Mankins, was a music professor, and Emily suspected that someday, Karen would be one, too.

Karen grinned. "Well, I mean, you would still be smart and nice and everything, but there's stuff you probably do now that's because of your parents, and maybe some of that would be different."

There were almost too many possibilities to consider. "I wonder if I would still love animals," Emily said. If, for example, her birth mother was allergic or something, and didn't have any around.

Karen nodded. "You definitely would. Your father would probably rather *not* have had pets, but you always wanted them, even when you were really little."

That was true. Her mother liked animals, but didn't *require* them, the way Emily did. As far as she could tell, her father had still never completely adjusted to the idea of pets running around the house and doing things like jumping on beds and sitting on the kitchen table, although he seemed to love Josephine and Zack a lot.

"I wonder if I would still like music," Karen said thoughtfully. "With, you know, the same parents as like, birth parents, but growing up with other parents."

There were no clear answers to that, either. "I don't know," Emily said. "You would still have *talent*, but if you had parents who never listened to music, I wonder if you'd still be interested."

"Predisposition," Karen said in her professor voice.

Maybe, yeah.

The bell rang, and they all filed out to the crowded hallway to go their second-period classes. In Emily's case, that meant Spanish, which she enjoyed, even though she sort of wished that she could have taken French, instead. French always seemed—elegant. From there, it was on to language arts, social studies, and then, lunch. The cafeteria usually had one vegetarian option—today, it was cheese ravioli—and there was a salad bar, too.

After lunch, she had math. Emily's pencil broke during the middle of her teacher's algebra lesson, and she hurried over to sharpen it, so that she wouldn't miss any notes.

The sharpener was right near the windows, and she glanced outside at the soccer and softball fields. Now that she was in junior high, they didn't have formal recess anymore, but sometimes, on nice days, they had gym class outside. But, she privately missed getting a chance every day to take a break in the fresh air, and run around a lot, and play games that weren't organized and almost never had *rules*. It seemed kind of arbitrary for schools to decide that recess was okay if you were in sixth grade, but much too childish if you were in *seventh* grade.

As she was gazing out the window, she flinched when a face suddenly popped up out of nowhere and stared at her with big brown eyes.

It was Zachary!

Ever since school had started, Zack had made a habit of coming to visit her regularly. Most of the time, she wasn't completely sure how he got out of the house, but he always seemed to manage to do it, somehow.

"Lassie!" someone in her class shouted, and everyone laughed. "Lassie came home again!"

It was a little embarrassing, but Emily was also happy to see him. "Is it all right if I let him in, Mr. Pennington?" she asked her teacher.

"Yes, he can stay in here until class is over. But, this really needs to be happening less often," Mr. Pennington said pleasantly.

Emily nodded. It was way too dangerous for Zack to be running around the streets all the way into town when he was looking for her.

Although Mr. Pennington probably just meant the interrupting-class-and-disturbing-everyone part.

She tugged the window open—the latch was stiff— and Zack climbed in clumsily. He jumped up to lick her face, wagging his tail, and then ran around the room to greet everyone else, including Mr. Pennington.

Emily got him settled down as quickly as she could, so that they could continue with the class. Zack yawned loudly and stretched out in the aisle, resting his head on her sneaker. Which made her feel as though it would be nice to have him go to school with her *every* day—but, that probably wasn't going to work.

Whenever Zachary appeared unexpectedly at the school, one of her parents would usually have to drive over, pick him up, and take him back to the college, where he would presumably spend the rest of the afternoon napping in one of their offices. Her mother's office was up on the third floor, in the political science department, and her father's was downstairs, in the history department.

After her math class ended, Emily guided Zack through the busy corridors and down to the main office. The vice principal, Mr. Kaufman, sighed when he saw them come in.

"*Again?*" he said.

Emily nodded sheepishly.

"How does he keep getting out?" he asked.

Emily shrugged. Sometimes, she thought he was just plain *magic*, since there really wasn't any other explanation that made sense.

"What is your next class, so I can write you a pass?" Mr. Kaufman asked.

"Science," she said. "With Mr. Strader."

After she called her parents, and her mother promised to come over right away, Emily sat down to wait. Zack sat on the floor next to her chair, leaning his muzzle on the crook of her elbow, and gazing up at her.

"I'm always happy to see you," she said to Zack. "But, you really need to stay home. It's not good for you to be running around by yourself."

Zack wagged his tail.

Emily had a sneaking suspicion that the only two words he had listened to were "happy" and "good."

They sat there for a few minutes, and she yawned. Zack immediately yawned, too, which made her yawn again. It was funny, how yawns were always contagious. But then, he suddenly perked up, looking very focused, and she instantly stopped feeling drowsy. Something must be going on, but she wasn't sure—wait, she could smell smoke. Or maybe Zack could smell smoke. Either way, she was sure that there was smoke—strong, acrid smoke—somewhere inside the school.

She jumped to her feet only about half a second after Zack did, and followed him towards the now-empty corridor.

"Hey, wait a minute!" one of the assistants in the office said. "Where are you going?"

"We'll be right back," Emily said quickly, and hurried after her dog without waiting for a response.

She sniffed the air, and was sure that it really *was* smoke, but she couldn't locate the source—or even the direction.

"Where is it, boy?" she asked.

Zachary barked once, and hurried down the hallway. He seemed to be leading her towards the cafeteria, and she picked up her pace, slipping and sliding a little as she tried to get traction with her sneakers. Bobby had a theory that the janitors always put extra wax on the floors in the school, just to keep people from being able to run in the halls without falling down.

Zack raced headlong into the cafeteria doors—which must have been locked, because when he rammed into them, they didn't budge. He panted uncertainly, and looked up at Emily for help.

Emily grabbed the handle, and shook the doors, but nothing happened. She was stymied, too, for a minute, but then remembered that there was another entrance outside, near the dumpsters and small loading bay.

"Come on!" she said, and ran for the main exit, with Zack loping right next to her.

She was going to get in really big trouble for leaving

the building during the school day—but, she couldn't think of another solution. So, they ran outside—right past a startled hall monitor—and Emily headed around the side of the building, towards the parking lot.

She pounded up a small flight of concrete steps, towards the metal door leading to the cafeteria's kitchen area. It was really heavy, but when she tugged it open, huge gusts of smoke came billowing out.

"Oh, wow," she said, and ducked instinctively.

Zachary tried to plunge through the doorway and inside, but she grabbed his collar to yank him back.

"No, it's too dangerous!" she said, using both hands to try and hang on to him and keep him from going in there.

There had to be a fire alarm somewhere that she could pull, but she didn't know where to look. The smoke alarm was blaring, so that was a good start, and maybe there was some kind of sprinkler system, too? It was a public school, so didn't there have to be equipment like that, for safety reasons? By now, with luck, people were probably already being given "this is not a drill" instructions over the intercom and starting to evacuate all of the classrooms.

In the meantime, Zack was still trying to twist away from her and get inside the kitchen, and she tightened her grip on his collar.

"No, Zack!" she said. "Stay here!"

She couldn't feel much heat, or see flames, but there was so much smoke that there had to be a pretty big fire in there. With the alarm blaring, help would be arriving any minute now, so she just needed to keep Zack safely out of the way, and wait for the fire department to take care of it. Maybe the smartest thing for her to do would be to run back into the school, and make sure that the principal and everyone else knew what was happening. But, the regular fire alarm was going off now, too, in addition to the cafeteria's smoke alarms, so she assumed that the news had spread to the rest of the school.

She backed carefully away from the smoke, feeling her way towards the little flight of cement stairs. The smoke was so thick that it was very hard to see what she was doing.

"The firefighters will be here soon, Zack," she said, her eyes burning from the smoke. "Come on, let's wait over there, out of the way."

Unfortunately, Zachary seemed to have other plans, because he wrenched free and charged into the building.

"Zack, no, it's too dangerous!" she yelled, as he disappeared into the smoke. "Come back here!"

But, as far as she could tell, he hadn't heard her, and there was no sign of him.

Now what? If she went in there after him, she was

going to get into a lot of trouble. But, he must have had a good reason for doing it, right? And could she really let her dog take a risk like that by himself?

Emily stood on the loading bay indecisively, not sure what she should do. Then, she heard Zack barking, sounding frantic. So, she closed her eyes, took a deep breath, and went in after him.

The smoke was so thick inside that she immediately started coughing and choking. It was also much hotter now, and almost impossible to see, although there seemed to be a bright orange glow somewhere up ahead of her. She had to feel her way along, and kept tripping, and banging into things. Counters, walls, chairs—she crashed into everything, as she stumbled along. It was scary, and she was going to turn around and run back outside, except that she wasn't even sure where she was, or how to find the exit.

She wanted to call for help, but it was too hard to breathe, so she didn't even try. She just pressed her shirt sleeve tightly against her nose and mouth, to try and keep as much of the smoke away as possible.

Then, she felt a large furry shape push against her left side. She felt for Zack's head, and then slid her hand down to his collar and held on tightly. There was too much smoke for her to try and speak, so she sent him the strongest possible image of them both running outside and breathing deeply in the cool green grass of the school's baseball field, just beyond the teachers' parking lot.

Zack noticeably hesitated, and Emily sent him the thought even more forcefully. They needed to get *out* of here, as quickly as possible. But, he kept pulling her forward, and she stumbled along behind him for a few steps. Then, he stopped short, and she lost her balance, falling over a long, heavy object that was spread across the floor in front of them.

To her horror, she realized that it was a body!

6

Emily was completely terrified—especially when the body moved slightly. But, that meant it was a person, who was partially conscious. A person who was still alive. It was starting to get so hot that it was hard to think clearly, and Emily could hear flames now—as well as the screeching fire and smoke alarms. The fire seemed to be off to her right somewhere, and the orange glow was brightening.

"Hurry!" she said to the person on the floor, and coughed, trying to get her breath. "We have to get out!"

The person was unresponsive, and Emily grabbed a limp arm to try and pull him or her away from the fire. There was no way she was going to be able to drag someone that big by herself.

Now, she felt Zack tugging at her sleeve, trying to guide her back towards the exit. He seemed to be determined to pull her away, which didn't make sense, when there was someone else who needed to be rescued.

"Zack, no, don't do that, you need to help me," she gasped. "We have to save the person!"

She was getting rapid mental images of being outside on the loading dock, and pointing at the building. She was pointing, and gesturing, and—okay, he wanted her to get help. She didn't want to leave the fire victim behind, but Zack was using his body to block her away from the fire, and force her towards the exit.

She closed her eyes, and imagined herself pulling the person's right arm, while Zachary used his teeth to grab the person's other arm by the sleeve. Then, she pictured the two of them working together to move the person safely outside.

She could feel Zack hesitate, and took advantage of that to stagger back towards the limp body on the floor.

Every single instinct she had told her that Zack *really* didn't want her to do that, but as she grabbed the person's arm, Zack did the same thing on the other side.

Then, she tugged as hard as she could, and felt the person slide forward a few inches.

"Good dog!" she yelled at Zachary. "Keep going!"

With both of them pulling, they made slow, but steady, progress. She stumbled and fell once, and Zack instantly was behind her, pushing her back up to her feet.

"Don't worry, I'm okay!" she said.

She fumbled around until she found the person's arm again, and resumed pulling. Emily wasn't really sure where the door was, but she trusted Zack, and assumed that he would be able to find the exit for them. The smoke didn't seem quite as thick now, and she thought there might have been a whiff of cool, fresh air somewhere nearby.

They got to the door just as several firefighters came barreling in, and they all crashed into one another. After that, everything happened very quickly, and Emily found herself out in the parking lot, coughing heavily. People were asking her if she was okay, and she nodded, looking around anxiously until she located Zack. He seemed to be all right, too, although his white fur was stained grey from the smoke.

It turned out that the person they had rescued was Mrs. O'Reilly, who was one of the school cooks. The paramedics were giving her oxygen, but Emily could see that she was sitting up now and moving around.

"Is she going to be okay?" Emily asked one of the firefighters.

The firefighter nodded. "It looks like she's going to be fine. You and your dog were very brave."

Emily shook her head. "No, it wasn't brave. We smelled smoke, and then I followed him, that's all."

The firefighter smiled. "Okay, if you say so. Now, let's get the two of you checked out by the EMTs."

Emily felt fine, but she let the paramedics give her some oxygen to breathe, anyway.

Her mother, who had just pulled into the parking lot, came racing over.

"What happened?" she asked anxiously. "Are you all right?"

Emily downplayed the whole thing, but her mother was quick to bundle her into the car and take her to the pediatrician. Luckily, the doctor said she was perfectly fine, but should maybe not run into any more burning buildings.

Which seemed like really good advice.

After that, they stopped by Oceanside Animal Hospital, so that Zack could get checked, too. While they were there, he also had the last booster shots for his yearly vaccinations. Their vet's name was Dr. Kasanofsky, but everyone in town called him Dr. K., for short.

"Well, he seems pretty good," Dr. K. said, after giving him a quick examination and listening to his chest with his stethoscope. "I don't think you have anything to worry about here at all."

"I'm going to give him a bath when we get home," Emily said.

Dr. K. nodded. "That's a good idea. Unless, of course, you *like* the way he looks with grey fur."

Emily laughed, imagining what it would be like if they just left him the way he was, so that he would have a whole new look.

"Any other great adventures this week?" Dr. K. asked.

Well, other than the hurricane, not really. "Just, um, normal stuff," Emily said. Her *new* normal, anyway, now that she had a *very special* dog.

They had to stop back at the school on the way home, so that Emily could pick up her knapsack and make sure that she had the right homework assignments. Everyone, from the principal, to teachers, to the firefighters who were doing a clean-up operation in the cafeteria, came over to praise her, and to pat Zachary. The fire had apparently started because some paper goods had been stored too close to the stoves. But, the good news was that Mrs. O'Reilly was going to be fine, although the doctors wanted her to stay overnight at the hospital, to be sure.

When they got back to the car, her mother looked at her for a long minute before starting the engine.

"Walk me through the part where you are sitting safely in the office, waiting for me to come pick up the dog, but then end up running into flames," she said.

Emily shrugged. "I don't know. Zack ran, and I ran after him."

"And," her mother prompted her, when she didn't elaborate.

"And, um, wrong place, right time?" Emily said. Or was it the other way around? "Right place, wrong time?"

Her mother looked at Emily, and then looked into the backseat, where Zack was cheerfully asleep, lying on his back with his paws in the air. "I'm very proud of both of you, but please *do not* do it again, okay?"

Emily nodded.

With luck, it was a promise she would be able to keep!

They finally got their power and phone service back on Wednesday, and Emily's main reaction was that she was really glad that she hadn't been born in pioneer times. A world with no television? No Internet? No refrigerators? It was hard to imagine. Maybe, if she had been born back then, she wouldn't have cared, because she wouldn't have known the difference. But, as far as Emily was concerned, living in the modern world was *way* better.

"Does it really count as 'roughing it,'" her mother had said, the night before, "if all three of us are sitting here reading our Kindles?"

"*Yes*," Emily and her father had said, without hesitating.

Anyway, with the electricity and everything back on, life felt much more normal. A couple of carpenters had come and installed new windows in her bedroom, so she could even sleep in her own bed again.

On Friday night, her grandparents flew up from New York City, and she and her parents drove down to Portland to pick them up at the airport.

As usual, her grandparents arrived with lots of packages and bundles. Her father always had cravings for things like "real" New York bagels and all, so her grandparents would bring him a lot of his favorite things to eat in big bags from stores like Zabar's and H&H Bagels.

On this visit, they had even more baggage than usual, because they were carrying a bunch of birthday presents, too.

"How is the birthday girl?" her grandfather asked, swinging her up into the air for a big hug.

"*So* mature that Mom and Dad are going to let me drive home," Emily said.

"Better you than me," her grandmother said.

Emily laughed. Her grandparents both knew *how* to drive—sort of—but, since they lived in New York, they didn't do it much, and didn't even own a car. When she and her parents went down to visit, Emily always enjoyed taking the subway, and she liked taxis even more. But, it was hard to imagine living in a place where you couldn't just go and jump in the car when you needed to go somewhere.

Her grandfather was such a nice and low-key person that Emily couldn't quite imagine him as a determined

Wall Street financial guy, but that was what he had spent the first half of his career doing. Then, he had retired, and started a small nonprofit agency to benefit poor families in the city.

Her grandmother had been an English teacher at a public high school in the Bronx, and even though she was really short, Emily had always heard that no one ever had the nerve to talk back to her in the classroom or give her any grief at all. She was constantly hearing from former students, who would usually say that, at the time, they thought she was too strict, but now, they were grateful, because it had helped prepare them so well. The school had been really sad when she retired, because so many of her students went on to college and interesting careers.

They had dinner at a fancy restaurant downtown, where every plate of food looked like it took about thirty hours to prepare. Then, they went to a movie which she and her father thought was really funny, but none of the others liked very much. Then, they rode back home for cake and presents.

Zachary and Josephine were waiting in the kitchen to greet them. This was the first time she had seen her grandparents since she had found Zachary, so they had never met him before.

"He is very—large, isn't he?" her grandmother asked, sounding nervous.

"A hundred and three pounds," Emily said proudly. He had been extremely thin when she first found him, and now he looked so healthy and strong!

"Goodness," her grandmother said, and blinked. The reason her father had never had a dog before was because his parents had never had a dog, either. "How much do *you* weigh these days?"

"Ninety-four," Emily said.

"Golly," her grandfather said, also eyeing Zachary uneasily.

Emily was relieved when, instead of jumping up and trying to kiss everyone's faces, Zachary sat down politely and raised his paw to shake hands. That seemed to make her grandparents feel much more comfortable with him. But then, when her grandmother put her purse down on the kitchen table, Josephine hissed loudly—and her grandmother jumped back in horror.

"She's not going to scratch you," Emily said quickly.

Probably not, anyway.

Zachary must not have liked it that she had hissed, because he made a low, critical sound in his throat—not a growl; just a canine comment—and Josephine promptly swiped her paw at him. He yelped, and leaped out of the way—which made her *grandmother* leap out of the way, too.

Her mother made a subtle motion with her head, and Emily nodded and picked up Josephine. Her cat complained rather noisily as Emily carried her out of the room and brought her upstairs.

"Gram really doesn't like cats," Emily said to her. "You shouldn't be mean like that."

Now that Josephine was in her arms, and had her full attention, she purred happily, and stretched out her paws. Her other grandmother—her mother's mother, who lived in California—would have said, "Butter wouldn't melt in her mouth."

Zachary trailed up the stairs after them, wagging his tail the whole way. When she set Josephine gently on the bed, Zachary jumped up there, too. This did not please Josephine, who smacked him on the nose with her paw. Even though he was about ten times bigger than she was, Zack whimpered and backed away from her. He retreated to the bottom of the bed, where he lay down miserably, resting his muzzle sadly on his paws.

Emily checked to make sure that he hadn't been scratched. But, as far as she could tell, the only thing that had gotten hurt was his feelings.

"You're all right," Emily said, and gave him a soothing pat.

Zachary just looked up at her mournfully.

"No, really," Emily said. "You're fine."

Josephine stalked around up near the pillows, whipping her tail back and forth, making it very clear that *she* was the superior animal, and *completely in charge*.

Emily imagined Josephine and Zachary sweetly cuddled up together—and was pretty sure that Josephine's reaction was along the lines of "Yeah, *right*."

"Okay, I'm going to go back downstairs," Emily said. "Try to stay here, unless you're going to be really, really calm."

Seeing her head for the door, Zachary jumped off the bed, landing on the floor with a heavy thump. He started to follow her, but halfway down the stairs, he stopped and his ears pricked forward.

Emily wasn't sure what he was sensing, but she did feel one thing very clearly.

There was danger somewhere!

Emily's first thought was the sickening fear that there might be another fire. But, no, she was feeling something else—a distinct hint of danger.

"What is it, boy?" she asked.

He was already bolting towards the back door, and she followed him, taking the steps two at a time.

When she raced into the kitchen, her father held his hand up. "Wait a minute," he said. "Where do you think you two are going in such a rush?"

"I, uh—" Emily had no idea, so it was hard to come up with a response. "Zack needs to go out, I think."

Since Zack was at the door, barking fiercely, that was probably pretty clear.

"Is it okay just to let him out?" Emily's grandfather asked.

Normally, one of them always went out in the yard *with* Zack, to make sure he was safe, but he was so eager to push outside that Emily wasn't sure it would work this time. Her grandfather opened the door, and Zachary raced outside, barking a deep, threatening bark over and over.

"He is certainly—rambunctious," Emily's grandmother said, nervously.

Emily thought she could see an image in her mind of dark shadows moving, but had no idea what that might mean. Dark, darting shadows, which looked sort of like people. *Sneaky* people. "I think we should call 911," she said. "It might be prowlers."

Both her parents, and her grandparents, looked startled.

"In the *country*?" her grandfather said. "There really aren't supposed to be any prowlers in the country. I'm quite sure of that."

The best way to find out would be to go into the yard and check for themselves. Emily started to open the door, but her mother pulled her back by her hoodie, holding the telephone in her other hand.

"No," her mother said. "Not happening."

Oh. Emily hesitated, not wanting Zack to be out there alone.

"*No*," her mother said, and quickly dialed. "Hi, Sonya, this is Joanne Feingold," she said, to the dispatcher who answered. "The dog is raising quite a ruckus, and I think there might be a prowler of some kind outside. Could you send a car by?" She listened for a moment. "Great, thank you," she said, and hung up.

Maybe someone was trying to break into the Peabodys' house, since they were out of town? But, no, Zack's barking seemed to be coming from the other direction.

Then, they heard a young male voice yelling, "Let's get out of here, dude!"

"Well, *that* sounds like an unruly punk," Emily's grandmother said, with a stern-teacher expression. She snatched up a tennis racquet that was in the corner of the kitchen, near the back hall. "I think we had better go check that out."

Emily's father sighed. "Mom, no. I really don't think that's a good—"

Emily's grandmother was already marching outside, gripping the racquet.

Emily hurried after her, with her mother and grandfather close behind. Her father was following them, too, but he was much slower on his crutches. Zack seemed to be down somewhere near Mrs. Griswold's house, which was boarded up, and in the process of being repaired from all of the storm damage. So, if someone wanted to break in, it wouldn't be hard to do.

"Exactly what is going on out here?" Emily's grand-mother called, in a voice almost as fierce as Zachary's bark sounded.

"Lady, call off your dog!" a young man's voice answered.

As they got closer, Emily could see two high school–aged boys up in a tree in Mrs. Griswold's yard, with Zachary barking below them. One of them looked sort of familiar, but she didn't think she had ever seen the other one.

"Come on, call 'im off," the other boy said. "We aren't doing anything."

"And so," Emily's grandmother said, "it just *happens* to smell like spray paint around here?"

Neither of the boys said anything.

Emily's mother had grabbed a flashlight on her way out the door, and she shined it on the house, where they saw words like "Witch!" and "Go Away!" spray-painted across the front. "Well, it looks like you two are going to have a lot of cleaning up and repainting to do, start-ing first thing tomorrow," she said calmly.

"No way," one of the boys said. "You can't make us."

"Maybe not," Emily's father, who had just caught up to them, said. Then, he pointed at the patrol car pulling up in front of the house. "But, *they* certainly can."

Once the two police officers, Officer Peabody and Officer Jarvis, had been told about what was going on, Officer Peabody waved up into the tree.

"Hello, Rex," she said. "Who's that you have with you?"

"My cousin Joe," one of the boys muttered. "Down from Bangor."

Officer Peabody turned to Emily's mother. "When does Mrs. Griswold come home from the hospital?"

"Tuesday," Emily's mother said.

Officer Peabody nodded. "Well, okay, then, that gives us a few days to get ready, then." She motioned for the two boys to climb out of the tree. "We're going to call your parents, and then go down to the station, and have a nice long talk about respect and good manners, and arrange for you and your cousin Joe to be *very busy* this weekend fixing this house up until it looks perfect. Understood?"

Rex and Joe nodded glumly.

"Come on, boys," Officer Jarvis said, opening the back door of the squad car.

When they started to move, Zack barked sharply.

"Emily, ask Zack to stand down, okay?" Officer Peabody said.

Stand down? Emily looked at her blankly.

Officer Jarvis smiled. "It means that he did a great job, but we'll handle it from here."

Oh. Okay. Emily nodded, and whistled once to get Zachary's attention.

He looked over, wagged his tail, and then sat down next to her.

"Good boy," she said, and patted him on the head.

"*Very* good boy," Officer Peabody said, and also patted him.

When the police officers had left with the two boys, Emily's grandmother shook her head.

"My goodness," she said. "We had to come all the way to Maine to see an actual *crime*!"

Emily's grandfather nodded. "That was very exciting. We *never* get to see crimes at home."

It was funny to think that they had to *leave* New York to find criminals.

When they got home, Emily's father actually locked the back door—which they almost never did.

"That was all pretty interesting," he said. "But now, I think it's time for presents and cake."

Emily certainly wasn't going to disagree with *that*.

So, they all trooped into the den, where her grandparents had stacked a bunch of brightly wrapped packages. She got totally great gifts from them, including various pieces of new hockey gear, all of which she immediately tried on. Starting in November, her parents had finally agreed to let her play hockey in a beginner's league, and she was really looking forward to that. She could already skate pretty well, but hockey was going to be an entirely new experience. Her father had asked that she please not be a goalie, so that he wouldn't have to watch people slam pucks directly at his little girl, and that seemed reasonable enough to her. Besides, it would probably be more fun to skate around, than to be stuck inside the net all the time.

"You certainly look fearsome," her grandmother said, sounding a little bit thrilled by the concept.

Emily nodded happily. Her helmet even had cool flames painted on it and everything! "I'm going to be a goalie," she said. "Dad's really excited about it."

"Ha," her father said.

Emily put in her new mouth guard and displayed her nicely protected teeth.

Her father nodded. "Just remember, you're never to go on the ice without that, no matter what."

Maybe she should start asking, *regularly*, how old she would have to be to take flying lessons, just to goof with him. Although suggesting *skydiving* lessons might be even better.

When the presents were all unwrapped, her mother

brought in a big spice cake with vanilla frosting, and everyone sang "Happy Birthday" to her. Josephine came back downstairs, and behaved very nicely, except for the part where she put her face into the ice cream carton.

It had been quite an eventful evening, and once Emily was in bed, she couldn't seem to fall asleep. So, finally, she decided to go downstairs and get a glass of milk. Josephine took advantage of this by moving up to sleep on her pillow, but Zack followed her to the kitchen.

They found her grandfather, who was famous for being a night-owl, sitting at the table, drinking coffee and reading the *New York Post*. As long as she had known him, he had always read several newspapers every day, including what he called "the rags."

When he saw her, he put down the newspaper and smiled. "Well, hello. You're not sleepy, either?"

Emily shook her head, giving Zachary a dog biscuit, and then sitting down across from her grandfather.

"I think we should have more cake," her grandfather said.

"I do, too," Emily agreed.

So, he fixed each of them a big slice, along with some ice cream that was probably full of Josephine germs, but Emily didn't mind, and apparently, he didn't, either.

"Thank you for all of the gifts," Emily said. "They're *excellent*."

Her grandfather laughed. "Your grandmother said that shopping for the gear made her wonder if she could find a senior hockey league somewhere and get out on the ice."

Her grandmother was not at all athletic—but, she was very determined, and she would probably be a good player. Emily *was* pretty athletic, but she didn't think of herself as being particularly competitive, so she had no idea whether she was going to be any good. But, her friend Florence was a total jock, and had promised to teach her how to play before the league actually started up.

"Is this Mrs. Griswold person actually that unpleasant?" her grandfather asked.

Emily nodded. "Yes. I mean, I don't think people should vandalize her house, or do any bad stuff like that, but she is really mean."

"I'd imagine she is very sad," her grandfather said.

Probably, yeah. "Zack likes her a lot," Emily said. "So, we're kind of friendly. I mean, she says hi to me and stuff, when we go by, and she never did before."

"Progress, then," her grandfather said.

"I didn't tell my parents, because I didn't want them to get upset, but she's the one who said they knew my birth mother," Emily said. "Then, she said no, I'm sorry, I made a mistake, I shouldn't have said that, and all. But, I guess she was telling the truth."

Her grandfather nodded. "Yes, I gather you all had a pretty rough conversation the other night."

That meant that one—or both—of her parents had been upset enough about it to tell her grandparents. In fact, they had probably told her grandparents on both sides of the family, and maybe her aunts and uncles, and some of their close friends, too.

"I didn't realize *how much* I don't know," Emily said. "And—" No, wait, she really didn't want to sound whiny.

"What?" her grandfather asked, when she didn't go on.

Okay. She sighed. "It makes it feel as though they care more about how *she* feels, than how I feel."

Her grandfather sighed, too. "I suppose it does, but you know that isn't the way it *is*."

She could know that like, intellectually, but that didn't mean that it felt that way. But, she nodded—mostly just to be polite.

"This isn't a situation with easy answers, Emily," he said. "We all have to feel our way through things like this."

Emily looked down at her cake, trying to decide whether she was losing her appetite, or just full.

"I have a feeling that twelve is a big enough birthday for you to feel more restless and impatient than you might have when you were younger," her grandfather said.

That was about the size of it, yeah. So, Emily nodded, reaching down to pat Zack, who was resting his head on her knee. "Are my parents upset that I wanted to talk about it?"

Her grandfather shook his head. "No, they're upset that they don't have better answers for you."

Okay. "Did you and Gram get to meet her?" Emily asked.

"No," her grandfather said. "I think she wanted to keep it very private, and that she was very young, and that it was all extremely upsetting for her. But then," he winked at her, "*we* lucked out, because we got to have you in our family."

Yes, she felt very lucky to be part of her family. "But, it's okay that I still have lots of questions?" Emily said.

"It's normal," he said. "And I hope that, someday, you get to find a few more answers."

Emily definitely hoped so, too.

"Time to get some sleep?" her grandfather asked.

Emily nodded. If anything, it was *past* time. And tomorrow, she was going to have her *third* birthday celebration.

Maybe turning twelve wasn't so bad, after all.

Because of the hurricane, they had had to postpone her birthday party, which was a whale-watching cruise in Casco Bay. But, the next morning, they drove down to Portland, and met ten of her friends on the dock where the boat was to depart. Most of the friends she had invited were people she had met at her elementary school, since she didn't know many of the people at her new junior high very well yet. So, it was Bobby, and Karen, and Florence, along with seven of her other friends.

Emily was a little disappointed that Zack couldn't come along with them, but then again, he really didn't enjoy being on boats. She assumed it was because before she found him, he had lived on a fishing boat—and his owners had been mean. If that happened to her, she probably wouldn't like to ride on boats, either.

They were welcomed aboard by a man who said his name was "Captain Bill," along with tour guides named Vince and Cara. Emily wasn't sure if they were all *really* required to wear life jackets the entire time, but she wasn't the only one with nervous parents. So, before they left the dock, they all suited up.

It was a warm fall day, the sun was shining, and the waves were nice and gentle. Some tourists were also on the cruise, so there were about twenty-five passengers, including everyone at her birthday party. Vince and Cara were stationed on opposite sides of the boat, each of them holding a microphone and narrating everything that they saw.

Which, so far, was absolutely *nothing* of interest. The tourists seemed pretty excited just to be in Maine, but all of the locals on the boat were looking around aimlessly, waiting for something exciting to happen.

"Well, these sure are nice seagulls," Bobby said politely, after they had been at sea for about half an hour.

"Very pretty when they fly," Emily agreed.

Their friend Harriet laughed. "You guys are so cynical."

Kind of, yeah.

Vince and Cara filled the dead air with fun facts about the history of Casco Bay, and the various marine animals and mammals they *might* see, but so far, they hadn't seen anything but seagulls.

"Look!" her friend Peter shouted as they passed some rocks. "A puffin! A real, live puffin! It's a miracle!"

Okay, they all saw puffins more days than not—but, still, they were fun birds to watch. They looked sort of like a cartoon version of penguins. And all of the tourists were very impressed by the puffin, and started taking photographs.

The boat operators were getting pretty frustrated that they hadn't seen anything unique yet, and seemed to be falling into some wishful thinking. Vince would announce, "I think we have a sea turtle on the port side!", and everyone would run over there, and then, the guy would end up saying something sheepish like, "Oh. I'm sorry. False alarm."

Since the cruise had been so uneventful, the boys started egging each other on, shouting stuff like, "Look, it's the creature from the black lagoon!" and "Sharks! Everybody, hit the deck!"

Emily thought they were kind of funny, but she also had a couple of stray moments when she thought that the next time she had a party, she just might not invite any boys. Even Bobby was being silly and immature, although he came up to her at one point and muttered, "We're maybe being jerks."

"Well, you should get them to stop throwing stuff," Emily said. "My grandmother hates that." In fact, she gave her grandmother points for not saying anything cross about it—yet.

Bobby nodded. "Yup. I'll tell 'em to dial it down a couple notches."

Good.

By the time they got to the small island where they were going to have lunch, they *still* hadn't seen anything exciting. But, they boarded small dinghies, and Vince and Cara rowed them to shore, promising to return to pick them up in about three hours. There were lots of little islands in the Bay, and all over the Maine coastline. Some of them had year-round residents, but some of the islands, like this one, were too small and had nothing but a few evergreen trees and rocks.

The picnic was really fun. Her parents and grandparents spread out red-checkered tablecloths on the sand. Then, they unpacked sandwiches and soda and juice boxes and chips and fresh homemade pickles her grandparents had brought up from a tiny store they always went to on the Lower East Side in New York.

Her mother had baked a small ham and made barbecued chicken breasts the night before, for sandwiches. She'd also baked some sliced tofu with the same barbecue sauce—which tasted a little strange, but was still good—and hard-boiled some eggs for egg salad. Her grandparents had brought up about eight different kinds of cheese, some of which they made into sandwiches with lettuce and tomato, and some of which was just cut into small chunks for snacking. Her grandfather was famous for his recipe for hot mustard, so they put that on some of the sandwiches, and homemade Russian dressing on some of the others.

Her father had recently bought one of those flip cameras, so that he could record Important Moments. He used it a lot, but they almost never ended up watching the videos, afterwards. He was also heavily into using his DSLR camera, and had Nikon film cameras, too. There was even a tiny little room in the basement of their house which he had set up as his own darkroom. Emily didn't like the smell of the chemicals, but sometimes she watched him develop them, anyway, because it was really neat to see the images appear out of nowhere.

After they ate, they played Frisbee, and looked for seashells and driftwood, and took pictures of "scenery." Emily thought it was pretty funny that every single one of them either had a small digital camera or a camera phone of some kind. It was like none of them went *anywhere* anymore without being able to capture it for posterity.

It was too steep and rocky for anyone to go swimming, but a few people took off their sneakers or sandals and waded a little.

On any other day, Emily would have wanted to sit quietly on a rock, and sketch—but, it would be dumb to be antisocial at her own birthday party. So, she threw one of the Frisbees around, and posed for not-very-candid pictures with her friends, and just generally goofed around.

When it was time for her cake, her mother produced such an impressive display—chocolate cake with cream cheese frosting, in the shape of a castle—that Emily suspected that her grandmother must have been the one who baked it.

Of course, she could also have guessed that, anyway, since she had smelled it cooking the night before. Being twelve was turning into the Birthday That Would Never End—which was pretty cool. At this point, she was on her third cake!

There were twelve candles, with one extra to grow on. Emily had always had trouble deciding what her wish should be—but, this year, it was easy. She wanted to learn more about her birth mother—and her birth father, if possible—and maybe even meet them. It didn't get much more simple than that.

She closed her eyes, took a deep breath, and blew out the candles with one hard burst of air. Everyone clapped, her father took a bunch of pictures, and her grandmother started cutting the cake and passing pieces to everyone. Naturally, Emily got the one with the frosted "E" on it.

Bobby requested the "B" from "Birthday," and everyone else who had an initial in the remaining letters—"Happy irthday, mily!"—ended up asking to have that piece, if possible. Which meant that Peter, and Harriet, and David, and Mikey, among others, were all pleased.

Her parents had planned ahead, and brought lots of trash bags, so that they could gather up all of their garbage and make sure not to leave any litter anywhere in the cove. In fact, they even picked up cans and plates and papers that some other group must have left behind.

Their timing was perfect, because they had just finished packing up when Vince and Cara appeared in the dinghies.

"I hope we see another seagull," Bobby said. "That would be so very neat."

Emily hit him with her elbow—but, also, laughed.

Once they were back on the ship, it turned out that the tourists had been riding around for three hours, without a single sighting of a marine animal or mammal of any kind. The tourists were still cheerful, but they looked tired, and as though they were more than ready to go home.

But then, finally, when they were halfway back to Portland, their luck changed.

"There we go!" Cara said triumphantly. "Look starboard, everyone!"

Since most Mainers knew a lot about boats, they all immediately focused on the water on the right side of the boat. The tourists and her grandparents weren't sure where to look—but, they caught on pretty quickly.

There were two whales cavorting out in the waves, and although part of her wanted to be a jaded local, Emily thought that that was *beyond* cool. They both even spouted little bursts of water from the tops of their heads, just the way they were supposed to breathe. In fact, it was almost as if they did it on cue!

Everyone was taking photos like crazy, but after one quick shot, Emily decided that it would be more fun just to enjoy watching them. She had always thought that the problem with cameras was that it was too easy to get all caught up behind the lens, and forget to have an actual *experience*.

"Pretty excellent," Karen said, standing next to her at the boat railing.

Emily nodded. "Yeah, we really lucked out. They're a lot bigger than I thought they'd be."

Captain Bill steered them in a few big circles, so that they could watch the whales for a while. Then, they resumed their steady chug back towards the docks.

Their guides looked visibly relieved when they also passed some seals sunning themselves on a rocky outcropping, and then saw a large sea turtle swimming by the boat. The cruise out to the island, with nothing but the occasional passing seagull, had made them extremely nervous, as far as Emily could tell. Her father had told her that the people who ran the tours had special sonar machines on the boat, to try and figure out where whales might be, but they had certainly come up empty during the first part of the trip.

Once they were back in Portland, they waited until all of her friends had been picked up by their parents, before they headed home themselves.

Her grandfather smiled at her. "That was fun, wasn't it?"

Emily nodded. "It was great! Just right for a birthday." She glanced at her parents since, obviously, they had paid for everything. "Thank you. I really enjoyed it."

"And I liked most of your friends," her grandmother said.

Emily laughed. "Do I want to know which ones you didn't like?"

Her grandmother blushed, since she probably hadn't meant to be quite that direct. "I don't think so, no."

"It was a nice way to spend a day," her father said. "We probably should have gone on one of those cruises years ago."

Emily nodded, since she completely agreed—and she hoped that they would go on another cruise sometime.

The only thing that would have made the day absolutely perfect would have been if Zachary and Josephine could have come along, too!

The next day was the Bailey's Cove Annual Kayak Races, and her mother was participating in the Women's Open category. She was a very serious kayaker, and belonged to two different local kayak clubs. She always got pretty keyed up before races, and she had been practicing even more than usual, lately. Most mornings, she got up long before Emily or her father did, and returned from her dawn workout around the time Emily was wandering sleepily downstairs to let Zack out and have some breakfast.

So, after a late lunch, they drove down to the big bridge—there were three different bridges in town, each of which connected a small island to the mainland—to watch the races. Emily cheered loudly when they saw her vet, Dr. K., win his age group, and come streaking under the bridge to the finish line, just about a foot ahead of the person behind him.

The races were fun and all, but after a while, staring down at the stream of kayaks started to get boring. Her mother's category wasn't likely to show up for at least another half hour, or maybe even longer.

"Dad, is it okay if Zack and I walk around a little?" she asked.

He nodded, fooling around with his tripod, since he had brought his big DSLR and his best lens to photograph the races. He was mostly just using a walking boot now, instead of his crutches, so he was having a much easier time getting around. "Sure. But, be careful, and don't go too far, all right?"

"We'll be right over there," Emily said, and pointed off to the side.

Her grandfather was busily playing around with the Flip camera, and her grandmother was having a long conversation with Bobby's Aunt Martha—who was a lobster boat captain, and always had great stories to tell. So, Emily figured they were both having a good time, and wouldn't mind if she wandered away for a while.

Zack was looking down at the rocks below the bridge and wagging his tail in a very friendly way. Emily assumed that someone they knew was standing over there, possibly doing some fishing, or trying to get a closer look at the races. But, when she looked over, she saw an unfamiliar elderly man.

He was tall, with stooped shoulders and grey hair, and his face looked as though he spent a lot of time outdoors. He had a gentle expression, although there was something very lonely about the way he was standing by himself on the rocks, staring out at nothing.

She didn't think it was at all cold out, but the man

was wearing work boots, dark wool pants, and a heavy plaid barn coat, with a white turtleneck on underneath. He seemed to be talking to himself, which made her suspicious, but Zack was still swinging his tail happily back and forth. Obviously, she trusted Zack's instincts—but she checked over her shoulder, just in case, to make sure that her father and grandparents weren't too far away.

"Hi," Emily said. "Pretty good race, isn't it?"

The man jumped. In fact, he almost seemed to *levitate*! "Are you talking to me?"

Well—who else? Emily took an uneasy step backwards, wondering why he looked so very pale. "Um, sorry. My dog just wanted to stretch his legs a little. We didn't mean to bother you."

He was looking at her as though she were some kind of alien being—which she thought was pretty offensive. It wasn't as though she was the *only* African-American person in Maine. She started to turn and walk away, but Zack sat directly in front of the man and lifted his paw.

To Emily's annoyance, the man stared at Zack as though *he* were an alien, too.

Of course, to be fair, he could just be afraid of dogs, maybe. But, it was hard to imagine anyone being afraid of a dog as sweet and friendly as Zack.

"You can see me?" the grey-haired man asked, still seeming completely unnerved.

84

It wasn't really unusual to run into someone kind of eccentric in Maine, but this man seemed to be a lot more weird than the average crusty New Englander. Emily checked over her shoulder again, relieved to see that her father was still only about thirty feet away. He was kind of distracted, since he was leaning over the edge of the bridge with his camera, taking shots of brightly colored kayaks zipping through the water. But, if she called him, she knew he would immediately hurry over.

"What do you see?" the elderly man asked urgently.

He was *much* too strange, and she was really starting to get the creeps from this conversation. "I'm sorry, we have to go now," Emily said. "My father is right over there waiting for us."

"It wasn't her fault," the man said.

Yeah, okay, whatever. Emily nodded politely, edging away from him.

Zack didn't want to cooperate, so she tugged a little harder on his leash.

"She needs to know that," the man said.

Emily nodded again, humoring him. "Okay. I'm sure it'll all be fine. But, we have to go." She gave Zack's leash another small yank. "See you around."

The man looked disappointed, but then, he turned away and started looking off into the distance again.

Emily hurried back to where her father and grand-parents were standing, feeling a little chill run up her back. Maybe Zack's judgment had been off this time? Because there was clearly something wrong with that man.

Her father smiled at her. "What were you and Zack doing over there all by yourselves?"

"We were just—" Emily stopped. What did he mean, *all by themselves*? "We were the only ones over there?" she asked.

Her father laughed. "Emily, there are some really good races going on. You've been missing some great finishes."

Emily glanced over the bridge railing and saw that, indeed, paddlers were still crossing the finish line, and that more categories must have already been completed, because there were a few kayakers standing on the main dock with ribbons and small trophies. Then, she looked back at the rocks, where the older man was still standing all by himself.

"Do you know him, Dad?" Emily asked, pointing.

Her father looked around. "Who?"

Wait, her father couldn't *see* him? Even though the man was right there? "Over on the rocks," Emily said.

Her father looked around in that general direction, and then shrugged. "Where?"

Oh, wow. Her father really couldn't see him. And the man had been startled that she and Zack could see him.

Whoa.

Double whoa.

Maybe even *triple* whoa.

She stared down at the rocks, trying to absorb all of this. Even though it was a clear and sunny afternoon, the man suddenly seemed to be surrounded by a small cloud of grey mist—and then, he disappeared!

"What's the matter, Emily?" her father asked, sounding very concerned. "You look as though you just saw a ghost."

She had a terrible, sinking sensation that that was *exactly* what had happened.

It made no sense at all, but she and Zack had apparently just had a conversation—with a real live ghost!

"Are you all right, Emily?" her grandmother asked.

"Yeah, I—" Emily shook her head to clear it. "Yes, I'm fine." She was tempted to say, Hey, I just saw a ghost! But, it probably wouldn't go over very well. She looked down at Zack, who seemed cheerful and relaxed, as though he saw ghosts every day and didn't think it was at all unusual.

Whoa, was it possible that he *did* see ghosts every day, and she had just never known about it? If that was true, she *still* didn't want to know about it.

"Hey, here they come!" someone yelled.

Everyone else moved over to the west side of the bridge, to see the contestants in the Women's Open category paddling furiously towards the bridge. Emily picked out her mother right away—the daisy decals on her helmet were a dead giveaway—and saw that she was fighting for first place with two other kayakers.

"Come on, Mom!" Emily yelled. "You can do it!"

She had no idea whether her mother could hear her,

but as the kayaks approached the bridge, they all ran to the other side to wait for them to reappear. And when they did, her mother was in the lead!

They all clapped and cheered and yelled encouragement as her mother's kayak sliced swiftly through the water, heading for the finish line.

It was the first time her mother had ever won the annual championship, and it was very exciting to watch her receive her blue ribbon and trophy. She had beaten some *really* good athletes, including a few women who competed in things like marathons and triathlons regularly. Her father took a bunch of rapid-fire photographs, and her grandfather captured everything on the little video camera.

Her mother smiled at her. "What do you think?" she asked, handing over the trophy so that Emily could hold it.

"That was *great*," Emily said. "*You* were great!"

It was fun to hold a trophy—a real trophy. When Emily had been in the Tiny Tots swimming class, everyone got a trophy, and the same thing happened in her soccer league. It didn't feel as special when a trophy was that easy to get. But, her mother had *earned* this one, by working hard and practicing a lot, and that made it really neat.

They went out for a celebration dinner, and then

drove down to the airport so that her grandparents could catch the nine-fifteen flight back to New York.

It had been a great weekend!

It wasn't until Emily had gone to bed, and the lights were out, that she had time to think about the other thing that had happened. It *had* happened, right? Thinking back, it was easy to wonder whether she had been imagining things, or whether her father just hadn't been looking in the right place, or whether the mist which had appeared to swallow the elderly man up was only a gust of unexpected fog.

Could it be possible that ghosts were *real*?! Well, okay, *she* was never going to be able to close her eyes and go to sleep again. They were supposed to be imaginary— not standing right there next to you, having a conversation, like it was totally normal.

Not that she was nervous, but since she sometimes had nightmares, her door was always left open a crack at night, so that she could see the light out in the hall. She got up, and opened it much wider, so that her room was barely dark at all.

Okay, good. That was much less scary. Because she was pretty tired, and she had school tomorrow, and staying awake all night wasn't a good idea.

Not that the elderly man had seemed scary, really.

He had mostly just seemed to be very, very sad. And Zack hadn't been scared at all; it had seemed as though Zack *liked* him.

But, Emily's last thought, before she dozed off, was that she *really* hoped that they never ran into him again.

Every weekend, her mother would spend a fair amount of time on the phone, trying to set up after-school plans for the upcoming week with some of her friends' parents. On days when Emily had her painting class after school, or went to an enrichment class or to watch her friends play a soccer game or something, it was much easier. She would usually be finishing up at about the same time one of her parents did, and so, she just got picked up in front of the school.

As far as Emily could tell, her parents were either the most strict parents she knew—or the most anxious. It didn't help that they didn't necessarily approve one hundred percent of Bobby, and that they really didn't like it when she went down to the marina to work on the boat. Her parents considered the fishermen and lobstermen "a rough crowd," for the most part. They would use words to describe them like "unruly" and "rambunctious," but what they meant was "unsavory."

But, today, they had agreed that she could get a ride home from school with Bobby's mother, stop by the house to check on Josephine and get Zachary, and then go down to the marina with Bobby to work on their boat project. The plan was that her parents would pick her up on their way home from work.

When they got to the boatyard, Bobby's Aunt Martha was busy repairing a big stack of lobster traps—and waiting for them. Emily assumed that her mother had asked her to chaperone them during the afternoon as much as possible. Her parents considered Aunt Martha impish and earthy, but very responsible.

"Now, remember, Emily, make sure you don't interact with any riff-raff, or let yourself hear any bad language," Aunt Martha said cheerfully.

Emily stared at her. "Did my mother actually say that?"

Aunt Martha grinned. "Well, maybe not those precise words. But, I made sure to curse several times during our conversation."

Her mother would have gotten the joke, of course— but, not necessarily thought that it was funny.

Bobby's boat had been completely destroyed during the hurricane when the Percivals' storage shed blew down on top of it. Because they had been almost finished, it was frustrating to have to start over. But, they had decided that they were going to build an even more ambitious boat this time. So far, they were building the new one a lot faster, and not making nearly as many mistakes.

Bobby got really mad if anyone in his family said that it might be good that the first boat had gotten wrecked, because the second one was going to be so much better. It was true, but Emily would never say anything like that herself, and she had been almost as disappointed about losing their original boat as Bobby had been. Okay, maybe the old one hadn't been as pretty and smooth, but they had worked hard, and she had enjoyed every minute of it.

Now, though, they knew exactly how to build a frame, and worked much more efficiently. They were better at sawing and sanding, too.

"What are we going to work on today?" she asked.

Bobby looked over the partial frame that they had already assembled. "Maybe sand the boards we're going to use for the seats?"

That seemed like as good an idea as any, so Emily reached for some sandpaper. They were building the boat the old-fashioned way, without fiberglass or pre-cut pieces of wood, so it took more work—but, it also felt like the boat was really going to be *theirs*, when they finished. It was the same way everyone in Bobby's family had *always* built boats, going back several generations. Most of the tools she and Bobby used had belonged to his grandfather, and probably *his* grandfather before that.

Zachary came over and sniffed the boat curiously, and prowled around a little. As far as Emily could tell, he was hoping that they were going to do something more interesting this afternoon. But, once he saw them start sanding, he sighed and flopped down onto a big beach towel she had spread across the ground for him.

She had been thinking about the ghost all day, but hadn't told any of her friends yet. Partially, because she was still trying to figure it out for herself, but also because she had been telling them *so many* peculiar things lately about being able to read Zack's mind, and stuff like that. She felt a little funny having to share yet another Very Odd Event in her life.

But, it was too big a secret to keep to herself.

"So," Emily said, as they sanded away. It was hard work, but the boards were going to be so nice and smooth when they were finished! "Something, um, really strange happened yesterday."

Bobby laughed. "What did Zack do this time?"

Well, that was the common thread in all of these adventures, wasn't it? "I think we saw—a ghost," she said, hesitantly.

Bobby looked up. "What? Are you kidding?"

"I could be wrong," she said, "but—I'm pretty sure it was real."

Bobby instantly put down his sandpaper and sat down to listen.

She told him the whole story, glancing at his expression every so often to see if he thought she might be nuts. But, no, he just seemed fascinated.

"That is so totally cool!" Bobby said enthusiastically, when she was finished. "Can I go see the ghost, too?"

It would be a lot better, for sure, if she weren't the only one, because then, it would all feel more normal. "I have no idea," Emily said. "He was really surprised I could see him. Like he was used to being invisible or something."

"But then he like, *materialized* in front of you?" Bobby asked.

Was that what had happened? "I'm not sure," Emily said doubtfully. "I thought he was a regular person. Especially when Zack went right over to him."

Bobby thought that over. "Would you still be able to see him, if you were someplace *without* Zack?"

Good question. Emily shrugged. "I never thought of that. Maybe." Plus, of course, when she went places, if it was at all possible, she liked to bring Zack with her, so it would be hard to test it out.

"Like, could he be standing here *right now*?" Bobby asked. "And we wouldn't even know it?"

That was a creepy idea. "I don't know." Emily couldn't help looking around, wondering if they were alone. She sure hoped so!

Besides, Zachary was sound asleep on his beach towel, which she assumed was a good sign.

"If he was here, Zack would probably go over to him," she said. "Or, at least, you know, *notice*."

They both looked at Zack, who was sleeping so heavily that he was snoring slightly. His paws weren't even twitching, the way they did when he was dreaming.

"While I was talking to the ghost, he didn't move around at all," Emily said. "I have a feeling he hangs out around the water, near the bridge."

"Maybe he was a fisherman or something," Bobby guessed. "So, he likes to be around the ocean and all."

That made as much sense as any other explanation. "Maybe he was lost at sea," Emily said. "And now, he likes to stand on the rocks, where it's safe."

Bobby nodded. "There've been lots of shipwrecks over the years. Did he seem like he was a pioneer or anything?"

Emily shook her head. "No, he looked just like, you know, a *Mainer*. Kind of outdoorsy, and his coat looked sort of like it came from L.L. Bean." L.L. Bean was a very famous store in Maine, with lots of camping supplies and winter boots, and the kind of outfits that people in Maine thought were fashionable, but most other people thought were just *preppy*—and old-fashioned.

"Can we go look for him tomorrow?" Bobby asked. "See if we can find out more?"

Emily wasn't sure she *wanted* to see the ghost— *any* ghost—again, but it would feel safer to explore with Bobby, than by herself. And it would be better to learn more details, instead of imagining all sorts of possibilities—including scary ones.

"Sure," she said. "Let's give it a try!"

10

Unfortunately, the next afternoon, Mrs. Griswold was being released from the hospital, and Emily's mother had offered to pick her up and bring her home. To be nice, Emily had said that she would come along for the ride. Mrs. Griswold apparently wasn't thrilled about the idea of not finding her own way home—big surprise—but, she must not have had any other options, because she agreed.

Once they got to the hospital, and all of the final paperwork was filled out, a friendly orderly named Robert brought Mrs. Griswold out to the curb in a wheelchair. Then, he helped her into the front seat of the car. She was going to be using a walker at home for a while, so he folded it up and put it in the backseat next to Emily.

"Good luck, then, ma'am," he said.

Mrs. Griswold nodded, staring straight ahead through the windshield. She had a stern expression on her face, but Emily noticed that she looked sort of tired, and small, and even older than usual.

"Thank you for the help, Robert," Emily's mother said. "We really appreciate it."

"No problem at all," he said, and turned to take the wheelchair back inside the hospital. "Take care now."

Once Mrs. Griswold had put her seatbelt on, there was a short silence.

"Well, okay, then," Emily's mother said, and started the car.

There was another painful silence, and Emily was definitely regretting having agreed to come along on this excursion. But, her mother always said that it was important to help people who needed help, even if they weren't very friendly about it. Her mother's theory was that those were the people who needed help the most.

As they rode along, there was no conversation, and Emily tried to think of something to say. But, Mrs. Griswold wasn't the kind of person who would think it was interesting to hear what she had done at school that day, or anything like that.

"Are you comfortable?" Emily's mother asked.

Mrs. Griswold nodded.

"I'm sure that hip is very painful," Emily's mother said.

Mrs. Griswold nodded—and maybe even winced.

They drove through Brunswick, where the hospital was located, and headed towards Bailey's Cove.

"Where's that dog?" Mrs. Griswold asked.

"That dog" sounded awfully hostile, but maybe she was just trying to start a conversation. So, Emily didn't snap "'That dog' is named *Zack*," even though it was the answer she wanted to give. "He stayed home," Emily said. "We were afraid he might get excited, and jump on you or something."

"Ah," Mrs. Griswold said.

It was quiet again.

After a minute, Emily's mother turned on the car radio, which was tuned to a classical station. Emily wasn't exactly an expert about classical music, but she thought it was soothing. On days when she had tests at school, her father often insisted upon playing Mozart at breakfast, because he said it would help her be able to focus better. She had never noticed any difference, but always said things to him later like, "Wow, that Jupiter Symphony *really* helped my math score!" and her father would say, "I think you're having a little bit of fun with me, Emily," and they would both laugh.

"You really don't like it when I call him 'that dog,' do you?" Mrs. Griswold asked.

Not even a tiny bit. In fact, she thought it was mean, and insulting. "His name is Zack," Emily said. "Or, sometimes, I call him Zachary. But, mostly, Zack."

Mrs. Griswold nodded. "Yes, of course. I will try to remember that." She looked over at Emily's mother. "It's very kind of you to do this for me, Joanne," she said, sounding as though she was having a hard time getting the words out of her mouth.

"We're happy to help," Emily's mother said. "And if you put together a list, we'll go out and pick up some groceries for you."

"Maybe we could just stop at Cyril's for a moment and get a few things," Mrs. Griswold said. "I really don't want to be a bother."

Emily thought that Mrs. Griswold mostly *liked* being difficult, but that she hated being obligated to people, or—horrors!—maybe even owing them a favor.

"How does the house look?" Mrs. Griswold asked.

It looked a lot better since those dumb high school guys had repainted all of the parts with spray paint on them, but Emily wasn't even sure if Mrs. Griswold knew that had happened. Probably, no one would have wanted to tell her about it, and she might not even have had any visitors in the hospital, except for Emily's parents. The last time Mrs. Griswold had seen the house, it had been severely damaged by the hurricane, so she must have been lying in bed in the hospital and worrying about that.

"I think they've done a good job with the repairs,"

Emily's mother said. "The water damage was mostly confined to the front room. The new couch was delivered already, but there are still a few other things you're going to need to replace."

Mrs. Griswold shrugged. "I'm not sure picking one out from a catalog was the best idea, but truth is, I never cared for the old couch. Samuel used to say—" She stopped. "Well, anyway, it was always too soft, and the springs were shot."

Samuel had been Mrs. Griswold's husband, who was killed in a car accident, when Emily was about a year and a half.

They had pulled into the parking lot at the Mini-Mart now, and Emily offered to go inside and do the shopping, while her mother stayed in the car with Mrs. Griswold.

Mrs. Griswold opened her purse, and handed Emily some money. "There you go, then. It's—very nice of you to do this."

It would be strange to be the kind of person who found it *hard* to say "please" and "thank you" and simple stuff like that.

Once she was in the store, Emily checked the list carefully, making sure that she got just the right brands, and amounts, since Mrs. Griswold would probably be cross if she made any mistakes. When she brought everything up to the checkout counter, Cyril studied the array of groceries.

"Well, looks like Abigail Griswold is home from the hospital," he said.

"How can you tell?" Emily asked curiously.

"Well, she loves those baked beans, and the brown bread," Cyril said. "And I've never seen your family buy light cream—it's always skim milk for your parents, and two percent for you. Plus, maple walnut ice cream is so unpopular that I really only stock it for her. The codfish cakes, too."

It must be pretty interesting to run a store, and get to know all kinds of things about the customers. Emily was pretty sure that Cyril had never sold tofu, until she became a vegetarian and her parents started buying it all the time. He probably stocked lots of special items like that, catering to specific people.

"I don't care for the woman," he said, as he packed up the bags, "but tell her that while she's laid up, if she calls in orders, I'll make sure they're delivered."

Emily liked to think that if their positions were reversed, Mrs. Griswold would do the same for Cyril—but, she kind of doubted it. On the other hand, although Emily had been too young to remember it, Mrs. Griswold had once been the mayor of Bailey's Cove for many years. So, at some point, she must have been friendly, and maybe even *nice*—although it was hard to imagine. After her husband died, she had resigned from her position, although Emily didn't know the details.

Once they were at Mrs. Griswold's house, Emily's mother parked as close to the front door as possible. Then, she set up the walker, and Mrs. Griswold eased herself painfully out of the car.

"Do you need help?" Emily asked.

"I can do it," Mrs. Griswold said snappishly.

Emily's mother instantly narrowed her eyes at Mrs. Griswold, who looked uneasy.

"I'm sorry, Emily," Mrs. Griswold said. "It is painful, and that makes me ornery."

"Don't worry, that's what I figured," Emily said, before she could stop herself. "Because you're like, *never* ornery."

"Emily!" her mother said sharply. "That's very rude of you. Please apologize right now."

Mrs. Griswold laughed. "Not untrue, though." She glanced at Emily. "I'll stop calling him 'that dog.'"

Mrs. Griswold might be a seriously cranky and unfriendly lady—but, she wasn't stupid.

"Thanks," Emily said. "And I'm sorry that I was, um, you know, snarky."

"Consider us even," Mrs. Griswold said.

It took a little while to get Mrs. Griswold into the

house and on her new couch, and Emily's mother fixed her some tea and a snack. She also made sure that Mrs. Griswold would be able to get around on her walker, and be able to take care of herself. Apparently, she had grumpily agreed to let a visiting nurse come by the house once a day, while she was recuperating, but she would still be on her own most of the time. So, Emily's mother was very worried about her.

Finally, though, they were back out in the car. Her mother let out a big sigh, before she started the engine.

"Mrs. Griswold sure seems to make things a lot harder than they need to be," Emily said.

Her mother nodded. "Unfortunately, yes."

"Do you think she likes to be that way?" Emily asked. "That it makes her happy?"

Her mother sighed again. "Not even a little bit," she said.

Emily's father was finally off his crutches, and just using a walking boot on his left foot, so he was the one who picked her up from school the next day. It was his night to cook, which always made him anxious and full of self-doubt—and Emily was relieved when he suggested that she take Zachary for a walk, so that he could think about his plans for supper.

She called Bobby, and he agreed to meet her at the

gnarled oak tree near the road to the bridge. He must have run all the way, because he got there before she and Zack did.

"Think we'll see the ghost?" he asked eagerly, when he saw her. He held up his digital camera. "If we *do*, I can get evidence."

"Or maybe all of the photos will be blank," Emily pointed out.

Bobby looked excited. "That would be even *more* cool!"

So, they walked down the road to the bridge, staying well to the side. Only two cars passed them, each of them being driven by people they knew, so they all exchanged waves.

"I looked on the Internet last night," Bobby said, "but I couldn't find anything out about ghosts around here. Except for lost sea captains, and settlers, and Native Americans, and soldiers from the Revolutionary War, and people who died from scarlet fever, and stuff like that."

Emily laughed. "That sounds like a lot of ghosts!"

"Well, yeah," Bobby agreed, "but none of them would have been shopping at places like L.L. Bean."

No, ghosts like that would be wearing homemade clothes, or uniforms, or deerskins and leggings and all.

Zachary ambled pleasantly along, not seeming to

think that anything about their walk was at all unusual. He was interested in seagulls, and chipmunks, and part of a hamburger someone must have tossed out a car window, but that was about it.

Emily paid very close attention to him as they approached the bridge. After all, he had been the one who was alert last time, and had made it clear that he wanted her to follow him down to the rocks. So, she would just follow his lead here, and trust that he would know exactly what to do.

Every evening, as the sun started to go down, the fog would usually start rolling in from the bay. Emily had always thought that it was really pretty, but right now, the fog looked sort of ominous and made the air feel chilly.

Was that a bad sign—or just a coincidence?

"Wait, there it is!" Bobby gasped, and pointed ahead of them.

Emily could see a tall, shadowy shape standing up on the bridge.

It must be the ghost!

11

Then, the fog cleared a little, and Emily saw that it was just Mr. Washburn, who lived about half a mile down the road. Mr. Washburn was a retired professor who spent most of his free time fishing—when he wasn't hanging out and drinking coffee at the Mini-Mart.

"Afternoon, kids!" Mr. Washburn called.

"Oh," Bobby said, and looked disappointed. "I mean, hi, Mr. Washburn."

Mr. Washburn was leaning against the bridge with his fishing pole in both hands, as he cast his line.

Zachary wagged his tail, and nosed at the big red plastic bucket next to Mr. Washburn. Emily could smell fish, but the scent was so incredibly strong that she assumed it was Zack's sensation, not her own. It must be pretty intense to have such a strong sense of smell all the time! Emily wasn't sure if she would like it.

"Have you caught much?" she asked.

Mr. Washburn shook his head. "Enough to cook up for some supper, maybe, but that's about it. Been pretty quiet out here." He grinned. "Of course, it's really *always* quiet around here."

Emily knew Bobby was dying to ask if Mr. Washburn had seen anything ghostly, but was managing to keep the words inside—so far.

But, that didn't last long.

"See anything weird today?" Bobby asked.

"Well, Mrs. Carleton drove by earlier wearing a *very* unfortunate hat," Mr. Washburn said.

Bobby's face fell. "That isn't all that weird."

Mr. Washburn winked at him. "You didn't see the hat, Bobby."

Zachary tugged her towards the rocks, and Emily let him lead her over there. Maybe he could see the ghost, and she couldn't this time? That seemed like a possibility. So, she would do her best to keep her mind very open to him, and try to pick up on his signals. But then, Zack just sniffed casually at the rocks, climbed around for a few minutes, and then pulled her back up to the road.

"Maybe the ghost is hiding, so that Mr. Washburn won't see him," Bobby whispered.

Maybe, yeah. Emily nodded.

They hung around for a while, but it seemed as though the bridge was just—an ordinary bridge. Nothing special, nothing unusual, nothing *haunted*. There were seagulls, and occasional passing boats, and gentle waves lapping against the rocks—but, that was it.

After Mr. Washburn caught one more fish, he deposited it into his bucket and began to pack up his gear.

"See you later!" he said, and waved a cheerful goodbye as he headed towards his house.

Emily and Bobby waved back.

"Maybe now, since the coast is clear, the ghost will come out," Bobby said.

Emily nodded. "I hope so. Maybe ghosts don't like to be around grown-ups?"

"Yeah, he'll definitely come out *now*," Bobby said confidently.

They waited, and waited, and *waited*—but, nothing happened.

A car or pickup truck would drive by once in a while, seagulls swooped around and cawed at each other, and the waves washed back and forth across the rocks. The most exciting thing that happened was that Zack found a piece of driftwood, and walked around in circles, carrying it happily in his mouth and tossing it up in the air every so often. But, that was it.

They both jumped when Emily's cell phone suddenly rang, although it was just her father, saying that she had been gone for quite a while, and that it was time to come home. Bobby's mother called Bobby about a minute later, and said almost the exact same thing.

"Guess we'd better get going," Bobby said. "Maybe the ghost only comes out once a year, or something like that. Like the moon and stars have to be aligned just right, maybe?"

Emily nodded. "Yeah. Or maybe it was a real person, and my father couldn't see him, because his glasses were fogged up, or he wasn't paying much attention."

Bobby nodded, too, and they walked along glumly.

"I was really hoping we'd see it," Bobby said.

To her surprise, Emily realized that she agreed with him. "Me, too," she said.

When she thought about it later, though, she was glad that it hadn't been a ghost, after all. Just being able to communicate with Zachary in a unique way was important and exciting. She really didn't need to be able to communicate with mysterious spirits, too. Her life was already complicated enough.

So, when she was walking Zack a couple of days later, and they ended up heading down the road towards the bridge, she didn't give it that much thought. In a small town, there were a limited number of directions she could walk in, and going over to the bridge was as good an idea as any other.

It was a very cloudy afternoon, and looked like it might rain soon. But, so far, she had only felt a sprinkle here and there. If it actually started raining, she and Zack would probably be able to make it home before they got completely soaked, as long as they hurried.

The closer they got to the bridge, the more eager Zack seemed. He kept wagging his tail, and looking up at her, practically dancing with excitement.

"He's there, isn't he?" Emily said.

Zack barked.

Which sounded a lot like a yes.

It wasn't too late to turn around, and she was tempted to do it, but Zack was moving forward with obvious determination.

"If he turns out to be scary," Emily said, "I am going to blame you."

Zack just wagged his tail.

The bridge seemed pretty deserted today, maybe because the weather wasn't very good. No one was fishing, there weren't any cars driving by, and there didn't even seem to be any seagulls around. But, somehow, Emily wasn't surprised to see the same man by himself on the rocks.

Zachary barked a greeting, and the man looked up.

Emily raised her hand to wave a tentative hello, and the man lifted his hand even more tentatively in return. He walked towards them, although it seemed almost as though he was *gliding* across the rocks.

He stopped about ten feet away from them, and they looked at each other.

"Uh, hi," Emily said.

The man nodded gravely. "Hello."

Zack didn't seem to think that any of this was at all unusual, and he sat down, raising his paw in a friendly way.

"That is a fine dog," the man said.

Emily nodded, since she certainly agreed with *that*.

"Why can you see me, when no one else can?" the man asked. "I've been trying to make contact for such a very long time."

Emily shrugged. "I don't know. I think it's because my dog can see you, and that makes it so that I can, too."

The elderly man frowned. "That is very strange."

"Very strange" was an understatement.

"Is this where you always are?" Emily asked.

There was a long pause.

"It's complicated," he said.

Well, *yeah.* "My friend and I were down here the other day, but you weren't here," Emily said. "Or were you—I don't know—invisible?"

There was another pause.

"It is complicated," he said.

That didn't answer her question, but he pretty obviously didn't *want* to answer it, or give her any details.

The only thing she could tell for sure was that Zack really *liked* the ghost, and wanted to be his friend. He kept going over to him with his tail wagging, and his head cocked to the side, waiting for a response.

"I have missed dogs very much," the man said, bending down to pat Zack. His hands looked as though they were partially transparent, but Zack seemed to be able to feel it, anyway.

That gave her a pretty good opening, then, to continue the conversation. "Did you have pets?" Emily asked.

He nodded. "Yes, and I miss my Marigold the most. She was a wonderful dog. But, she has also been gone for a very long time."

Okay, that totally wrecked one of the things she had always assumed happened during an afterlife. "You don't get to see her?" Emily asked. "I mean, um, where you are?"

Wherever *that* was.

He shook his head wistfully. "She moved on, at once. Animals have very beautiful souls."

It was still very disappointing. "I always thought

114

that if something happened to you, your animals were supposed to be there waiting for you," Emily said.

"And so she is," he said. "As are many others. But, I must finish my work, first."

This was all way too confusing. It might be better if she just hadn't asked at all.

The man must have picked up on that, because he smiled at her. "You don't need to worry, my young friend. Everyone is on a different journey. Each of us finds his or her own way."

"Aren't ghosts supposed to—go someplace else?" she asked. "A different dimension, or something?" Her family went to church and all, and she was mostly Episcopalian, but her father was Jewish, and sometimes, they went to synagogues, too. Emily had been going to Sunday school classes for years, but she was starting to wonder if she had been paying enough attention. Her parents had talked about God, and religion, and different ideas, too, but Emily wasn't completely sure what she believed, especially about things like the afterlife.

"I cannot leave," the man said, "until I finish."

Weird. "Um, finish *what*?" she asked.

"Peace," he said.

Wow! "World peace?" she asked. If that was his job, he was maybe going to be busy for a *really* long time.

"I need to put things at peace," he said.

Well, there was no reason that ghosts were necessarily supposed to make *sense*. It might even have been disappointing if an encounter with a real ghost wasn't kind of cryptic, but at least, it would have been easier to understand. Maybe she would ask him something more basic. A question with a concrete answer might be the best choice. "How long have you been here?" Emily asked.

"I don't know," the man said. "Time is slow, and fast. What day is it?"

Standing here talking to a ghost, like it was normal—while she threw sticks for Zack to fetch—was maybe making her feel a little nuts. A situation like this shouldn't seem ordinary. "Friday," she said.

That answer clearly made no sense at all to him. "Is it autumn?" he asked.

She nodded. "October." Oh, wait, maybe that's what he meant by "day." "October sixteenth."

"What is the year?" he asked.

For some reason, that was the sort of thing she would have expected a ghost to know. Not that they would be reading newspapers or whatever, but shouldn't they have inside information? Maybe nothing worked at all the way she had imagined that it would. "2012," she said.

He looked shocked. "Are you sure?"

Of course she was, but for a second, she suddenly doubted herself. "Well—I think so," Emily said. "I mean, yes. Definitely."

"I have been gone for longer than I thought," he said softly. "Much, much longer."

It would probably be rude to say something like "So, uh, when did you die?" But, it was the obvious question. She was afraid to ask it, though, since she would sound completely tactless.

"I would have thought that after so much time—" The man stopped without finishing his sentence. "I'm sorry, I must go now."

And with that, he disappeared again!

Emily tried not to make it obvious during dinner that she was completely distracted and finding it very hard to concentrate on the conversation—or her food. At least Zack, who kept nosing at her plate the entire time, wasn't having trouble paying attention to food! Then again, hanging out with a ghost didn't seem to bother him at all, either.

Since her father had cooked the spaghetti, her mother did the dishes, and Emily helped her. Then, after her homework was all finished, she went into the den to watch television for a while.

Her father was already in there, reading the newspaper.

"Is it okay if I turn that on?" Emily asked, gesturing with the remote control.

"Sure," her father said. "Although I like shows better when they aren't about high school students who all look thirty years old."

Emily laughed and put on a sitcom that was usually pretty funny. Josephine immediately got up on the couch and curled onto her lap, while Zachary stretched out on the floor, resting his head on her sneaker. Emily really liked the way her pets seemed to enjoy spending time with her as much as *she* enjoyed spending time with them.

"Have there ever been any shipwrecks near the bridge?" she asked, when the first scene of the show ended and some commercials started.

Her father glanced up from the article he was reading. "Which bridge?"

Bailey's Cove had three main bridges—the cribstone bridge, which had been built with a complicated arrangement of stacked stones and was a famous landmark in town, the "big" bridge, and the "little" bridge. "The big bridge," Emily said.

Her father shrugged. "I don't know, maybe. We could do some research about it, if you want. Do you have a project for school?"

Emily shook her head. "Not really. I was just curious." As a history professor, her father was usually very good at remembering even the most obscure stories about past events. "Has anyone ever drowned there? Maybe someone who fell off the side and into the water?"

"Possibly," her father said, sounding as though he was only half-listening. "But, not that I remember."

Emily grinned at him. "Well, you *are* from away." Which was how all of the locals described *anyone* who hadn't lived in Maine for several generations. Since her parents were from New York and California originally, they were considered even more "from away" than most non–Maine natives.

"And they'll never let me forget it," her father said wryly. He picked up his newspaper again. "But, no, the only thing I can ever remember happening on the big bridge is the terrible accident years ago."

Emily had been drifting off a little, but she perked up when she heard that. "What accident?"

"The car accident the Griswolds were in, when poor Mr. Griswold was killed," her father said.

Wait, was it possible that the ghost was *Mr. Griswold*? No, that would be too weird. Besides, he seemed *nice*, so that made it even less likely. She would expect Mrs. Griswold's husband to be as unpleasant and difficult as she was. "It happened on the bridge?" she asked.

Her father nodded. "They were on their way home,

and they hit some black ice, went through the wooden barrier, and ended up down on the rocks. The whole thing was really awful. It wasn't anyone's fault, but if you were behind the wheel, I think it would be very hard not to feel that way."

Wow. There were lots of rumors around town, of course, but she had never heard those specific details before. Or maybe she had, but just hadn't been paying attention?

"Jim Peabody called me, and we went down to try and help, but there wasn't much we could do." Her father shuddered. "That was a terrible night."

It must have been, and Emily was glad that she hadn't been there. "Mrs. Griswold was driving?"

Her father nodded.

Okay. That meant that Mrs. Griswold had been blaming herself for all of these years—and maybe that was why she was so mean? "So, she changed after that?" Emily asked. "And wasn't friendly anymore?"

Her father waved his hand in a "no, not really" motion. "I don't know. She certainly always had a strong personality. But, she wasn't antisocial, and she never had trouble getting re-elected whenever she ran for mayor."

That still didn't seem possible, but Emily's mother had always described her as "a superb administrator," so that might be why she had been re-elected so many times. "Were she and Mr. Griswold happy?" Emily asked curiously.

Her father shrugged. "They certainly seemed to be."

Which must be why, so many years later, Mr. Griswold was still unable to be at peace.

Somehow, she and Zack had to figure out a way to help him!

Emily was eager to go back to the bridge, and see if the ghost really was Mr. Griswold, but she didn't get a chance the next day because they already had plans. First, they raked some leaves in the yard, and then they drove over to the college to go to a home football game. They had season tickets, and *never* missed a game. Football wasn't Emily's favorite sport, but she liked going, because the people in the stands got so excited, and shouted and clapped and cheered every play, and it was fun to be part of that.

Over the years, she had actually learned a lot about the game, and could now usually predict when the team was going to pass or run, and could sometimes even recognize different kinds of defenses.

They also regularly went to college basketball, hockey, softball, and baseball games at Bowdoin. Her mother liked—and had played—just about every single sport that existed, so she would go watch anything, including boring stuff like golf. Emily's father played tennis once in a while, but when it came to sports, he mostly preferred just being a spectator.

Emily leaned in the direction of being a spectator herself, although a pretty *active* one, because she enjoyed sketching whatever kind of game they were attending. It was really hard to capture movement on the page, and she liked the challenge of trying to draw someone leaping for a ball, or diving for a goal, or whatever else might be happening.

She had tried playing lots of sports, because her parents wanted her to be "exposed to new things." She didn't mind soccer, since it was an excuse to run around like an idiot for an hour, but the game itself didn't do much for her. She had been taking swimming lessons at the college for years, with other faculty kids, and she wasn't a star, but she was good enough to have been promoted to Level 5 as a swimmer, and was now working on her Level 6 skills. She didn't think she ever wanted to be a lifeguard or anything, but it would be nice to be *qualified* to do that.

Tennis was fun, but she wasn't very good. She didn't mind playing catch in the backyard, but other than that, baseball and softball were more fun to *watch*, in her opinion. Especially, of course, the Red Sox.

Bowdoin won the football game, so everyone left in a good mood. A couple of professors her parents knew were having a post-game cookout, so they went to that. Emily always tried not to make a big deal of being a vegetarian, since it sometimes made people uncomfortable, but Dr. Bougainer made her a thick grilled cheese and tomato sandwich—without even being asked—which Emily thought was really nice. She had two ears of corn and some salad, too.

Then, on Sunday, they went to church in the morning. They had to get there more than an hour early because Emily had her religious education class at ten, and her mother had choir practice. As far as Emily knew, her father was going to wait in the car, with a book and some coffee, until it was time for the eleven o'clock service.

There were a few friends who she usually only saw at Sunday school, because they went to private schools or were home-schooled. So, it was fun to talk to them, and find out what they had been doing all week. Seeing them in person was a lot better than exchanging messages online and stuff like that.

She always had lots and lots of questions during the actual classes. But, she would only ask a few, because the teachers would usually end up looking tired, and say things like, "Well, that's the nature of *faith*, Emily" or "It's meant to be a parable, that's all."

After church, there was often a reception in the

courtyard, or in the church hall, with coffee and hot cider and homemade cookies and all. Any teacher her parents encountered would invariably laugh nervously and say something like, "Your Emily is certainly an intellectually *curious* child, isn't she?"

Her parents would look very pleased—which always seemed to disappoint the teachers, who seemed to be looking for concerned, and maybe even alarmed, reactions.

That particular day, they spent the class session discussing ethical dilemmas of various kinds, and different choices they could make if faced with complicated situations. Like, what should they do if they saw one of their friends cheating in class, or knew that they had plagiarized a homework assignment. Emily had had a bunch of "Well, what if . . . ?" variations, which might change the details ever so slightly, but that didn't seem to be the way her teacher, Mrs. Mulligan, wanted the conversation to go.

She also had a *stack* of questions she wanted to ask about the afterlife, but didn't have the nerve to turn the conversation in that direction, and wreck Mrs. Mulligan's lesson plan.

"What unanswerable questions did you ask today?" her father wanted to know, when they were standing around at the reception after mass, eating snacks.

"I asked her why, no matter how much pitching the Red Sox have, it's never enough," Emily said, and both of her parents laughed.

"Did she have an answer?" her mother wanted to know.

"Fatally flawed bullpen," Emily said, and her parents laughed again.

When they got home, it was such a warm day for October, that they spent the entire afternoon out on their deck. Her parents worked on their lectures for the upcoming week, and corrected midterms and papers, while Emily finished up her homework. By the time she was done, her parents were both still busily working away.

"Is it okay if I take Zack for a walk?" she asked.

"Sure," her mother answered. "Just don't go too far, and bring your cell phone with you."

"Takeout Indian food sound good for tonight?" her father asked.

Emily nodded, since takeout Indian food *always* sounded good to her.

Naturally, she walked Zachary down to the big bridge. Because it was a nice day, there were a lot of people out on the water in sailboats and kayaks and canoes. A few other people, including Mr. Washburn, were fishing, but since it was late in the afternoon, most of them were starting to pack up their gear.

There was no sign of the ghost, and she wondered if he was gone for good. But, it seemed more likely that he really didn't want to be visible when other people were around. Until she and Zack had been able to see him, he must have assumed he could appear whenever he wanted, without being noticed, but she had a feeling that he was a lot more cautious now.

So, she and Zachary crossed the bridge and wandered around aimlessly for a while. Zack fetched some sticks; Emily skipped some rocks in the cove. When they walked back, the fishermen had all gone, although a few pleasure boats were still drifting by, on their way in for the night.

"I don't see anything," she said to Zack.

Zack gave her what *looked* like a dog shrug.

"We can't summon him, I don't think," Emily said. "It just seems to happen."

Or not happen, depending.

They stood around for a few more minutes, before Emily decided to give up.

"Let's go home," she said to Zachary. "Mom and Dad will want to eat supper pretty soon."

Zack followed her agreeably. But, as they were passing the rocks, he stopped and cocked his head. Emily could tell he was already seeing something, but it took a minute for the ghost to come into view for her.

"Good boy," she said, giving him a pat. "You are very, very smart."

Zack wagged his tail, clearly pleased by the compliment.

Emily knew that the ghost could see *them*, but wasn't sure if he knew that it went both ways.

"Hi," Emily said. "We wondered if you would be around today."

The ghost smiled at them. "I am pleased to see you again, young lady."

"I'm Emily," she said. "I mean, you can call me that. And this is Zachary, although he likes Zack, too."

The ghost nodded solemnly. "Thank you, Emily." He shook the paw Zack offered. "And hello to you, Zachary."

Zachary barked in response.

Should she ask—or pretend to have no idea? "I'm not sure if I'm allowed to know," Emily said, "but, are you Mr. Griswold?"

The ghost stared at her with amazement. In fact, if he weren't *already* a ghost, she would have said that he looked as though he had just seen one. "You know of me?" he asked.

"I was just guessing," Emily said. "It seemed to make sense."

He looked worried. "Have you spoken of this to others?"

It was probably impossible to lie to a ghost; they must have access to inside information. "My friend Bobby," she said. "But, I hadn't figured out who you were yet, so we just talked about me seeing a—well, you know, *ghost*."

"Was that the young lad who was with you before?" Mr. Griswold asked.

Emily nodded. "He really wanted to see you, but he didn't take it personally."

"I don't even know why you and your fine canine are able to see me, when no one else can," he went on. "But, I think you are the vessels to allow me to communicate my message."

Emily's Aunt Patty, who lived in California, was into a lot of New Age stuff, which she described as being "spiritual." Emily's father described it as being "too much time in all of that ridiculous California sunshine." The other-worldly things Aunt Patty talked about had always seemed very mysterious to Emily, and even kind of *silly*—but, maybe there was something to it.

"Do you want us to talk to Mrs. Griswold?" Emily asked. "Tell her we saw you, and you're okay?"

Again, the ghost looked aghast. "These things are not that simple, child."

"Why?" Emily asked curiously.

"We must *never* cause pain," he said. "Or turmoil."

Okay. It sounded like this ghost stuff was maybe more convoluted than it needed to be, though. On the other hand, what were the odds that, if she told her, that Mrs. Griswold would believe her, anyway?

Maybe she shouldn't ask this, but she couldn't resist. "Is it scary? Where you are? Or really boring, because it's been a long time?"

He shook his head. "I have my task."

That wasn't really a clear answer. "Did you see a white light and everything? And wake up someplace beautiful?" she asked. "And now, do you sort of, I don't know, *commute* back and forth?"

He smiled kindly at her. "There is much that can't be explained. Time, and space—I have no words to describe it."

"Are you *allowed* to explain stuff like this? To—" She didn't know how to describe herself, in this situation. "Well, you know, civilians?"

He smiled again. "Everything is revealed at the right time."

Maybe, when he was alive, *he* was the one who should have been a politician, instead of his wife, because he sure was good at avoiding giving straight answers. "But, there must be some reason Zack and I can see you," she said. "It can't be like, you know, just *random*."

He nodded seriously. "It seems as though you two are destined to help."

"How?" Emily asked.

"All is not known," he said. "It seems that you and the noble animal will serve as the bridge. That is all that I know."

She had met some kind of boring professors over the years, but Mr. Griswold spoke in an even more stiff way than they did. "Were you all formal and everything before?" she asked.

He looked confused.

"The way you speak," Emily said. "It's—well—unusual."

He nodded. "Ah, I understand. Language is different for me now. It is not easy to find words you will understand."

She still had about a trillion questions she wanted to ask, but it didn't seem as though he was going to be able to answer them, or even if he *could*. "Are there things Zack and I are supposed to be doing? To help out?"

"Soon, I think," Mr. Griswold said.

Maybe it was better just not to think too much about what all of this meant. Mr. Griswold was—the reasons didn't matter, really—able to communicate with them. And, as far as she could tell, the only other important thing was that he needed their help to figure out a way to make Mrs. Griswold able to accept the fact that he was gone, and stop blaming herself.

There wasn't much point in trying to make it any more complicated than that. And, hey, the whole thing was *already* pretty complicated.

Mr. Griswold looked up at the sky, as though he could hear something. "Ah," he said, and nodded to himself. "At this time, I must bid you two farewell."

With that, he faded away, and Emily found herself standing alone on the rocks with Zack. Then, she suddenly felt very hungry—for a big bowl full of chopped meat.

Yuck. But, it was heading towards sundown, and Zack was obviously ready for his dinner.

"Time to go home and get some food?" she asked.

Zack started bounding across the rocks, pulling her towards home.

Emily laughed, and followed him. "I think I'll take that as a yes," she said.

They were just starting down the dirt road towards their house, when Zack started to act—twitchy. Since he was so much more sensitive than she was, Emily looked around to see what might be wrong. It would be nice, of course, if it wasn't another ghost. Then again, maybe it was just Mr. Griswold coming back to tell her something?

"Hello?" she called out cautiously.

"Help!" someone responded. "Down here!"

Down where? She could hear the voice, but she couldn't locate it.

But, Zack was already pushing his way through the bushes on the side of the road. When she looked more closely, Emily could see that a lot of the branches were already broken.

The ground was very steep and rocky, but she could see flashes of bright colors at the bottom of the slope. She recognized Kurt, Bobby's father's regular sternman on his lobster boat.

He must have been riding his bike, and skidded out of control or something, because he was lying in a twisted heap of metal, bicycle wheels, and branches. The bright colors she had seen were the orange-and-yellow fluorescent–colored biking clothes he was wearing, along with a shiny red helmet.

"Are you okay, Kurt?" she asked. "What happened?"

"Spun out on some gravel," he said glumly. "I think I might have busted my leg."

She saw the angle of his lower leg—and felt a little sick to her stomach. "I'm sorry," she said. "It looks like it really hurts."

"Yeah, it feels pretty bad." Kurt sighed. "I'm going to be looking at about two months of not being able to ride. But, I sure am glad I had the helmet on."

She was, too.

Zack was trying to drag branches away from the area, so that they could pull Kurt free, but Emily put her hand out and motioned for him to stop. "It's okay, boy," she said. "We'll call for help—it's easier."

"Thanks, Emily," Kurt said, as she took out her cell phone. "My gear must have gone flying all over the place when I was tumbling down the hill."

That meant that she could give Zachary something to do, so he wouldn't be bored while they waited for the ambulance to arrive. "Was it just a cell phone?" she asked.

Kurt shook his head. "It was one of those belts that holds water bottles, and food, and have a pocket to zip your keys and phone inside."

The description was clear enough for Emily to re-member having seen him wearing it before, when he biked past her on his regular rides, and she was pretty sure that the pack had been made of blue canvas. She closed her eyes, picturing the waist pack. Then, just for cover, she turned to Zack, who was already alert.

"Fetch Kurt's bag, please, Zack," she said.

She was pretty sure that the word "fetch" didn't mean much to him, even though chasing after balls and sticks was one of his favorite ways to spend an afternoon. But, she pictured the blue pack as vividly as she could, including the image of Zack diligently searching the underbrush to try and locate it.

"Find the pack, boy," she said. "Good boy!"

Zack barked, and then started snuffling around through the leaves and dirt.

"He's awfully smart," Kurt said, with obvious admiration. "Maybe you should sign up for some classes, and train him to be a Search-And-Rescue dog."

When it came to that, Emily was pretty sure that Zachary wouldn't *need* much training. Now that Zack was occupied, she quickly punched "911" into her keypad, so that she could report the accident and their location.

The dispatcher who answered was Sonya Hargrove, who also worked at the hair salon on weekends, in addition to her job at the Bailey's Cove Police Department.

"Okay, hun, the paramedics are on their way," Sonya said, once Emily had described what had happened. "They should be there in about ten minutes. Tell Kurt to hang on a little longer." Then, before she hung up, she changed the subject abruptly. "How's that conditioner I ordered working out for you?"

There wasn't much demand in town for African-American hair-care supplies, but Sonya had done some research and put in a few special orders.

"Pretty well, thanks," Emily said. "Especially when I leave it in overnight."

"Glad to hear it," Sonya said. "I emailed a few of my colleagues, to see what they thought, and they all agreed that those would be the best products for us to stock for you."

There was the sound of another telephone ringing in the background.

"Oops, there's another one! I need to take that, hun," Sonya said. "You and Kurt just sit tight. The rescue squad's ETA is down to about six minutes now."

With all of the emergencies she had been around lately, Emily had finally looked it up on the Internet one night and found out that ETA meant "Estimated Time of Arrival."

Since Kurt was a lifelong fisherman, six minutes was more than enough time for him to tell her about the time he had been on a swordfish fishing trip, and he and his shipmates caught an eight-hundred-pound unidentified scaly fish with huge, folded-up wings and long fangs. They had all been sure that the fish was a holdover from prehistoric times, and that it could probably fly, and maybe even breathe fire.

Emily had learned when she was very small that local fishermen were famous for telling tall tales that couldn't possibly be true, but were always entertaining. So, she was happy to sit down on an old tree trunk and listen. Snacks were always an excellent idea, and she found a granola bar in her pocket, which she split in half, and she and Kurt shared it.

"And then," Kurt said, deep in the story, "four more of them rose up out of the sea, twenty feet long, if they were an inch! They flapped their wings like madmen, and caused a wind strong enough to push our boat off course. The waves whipped up all around us, and we were sure that we were going to be swamped."

Just then, Zack came charging out of the bushes, proudly carrying Kurt's waist pack in his jaws.

"Well, how about that," Kurt said. "You have a seriously smart dog there, Emily!"

Yep. He was the best dog ever, and Emily gave him a small biscuit she had found in her pocket.

Kurt was in the middle of describing the piercing shrieks the prehistoric bird-fish had made, and the way their fangs gleamed in the moonlight, when the rescue squad arrived.

Emily watched as they carefully extricated him from the tangle of mangled bicycle, put an air-splint on his lower leg, and strapped him into one of those metal rescue baskets. Then, they hauled him safely up the slope, to the dirt road, where they transferred him to a gurney.

"Oh, this is terrible," Kurt said sadly. "I'm not going

to be able to tell you what happened next, when we began using our shovels as swords, and confronted the dinosaur fish."

Emily grinned. "You can finish it the next time I see you down at the boatyard."

"Wait until I tell you about the giant spiny sea urchins that started hovering over us!" Kurt shouted, as the EMTs closed the back door of the ambulance.

Since it was going to be dark soon, the police gave Emily and Zack a ride home in one of their squad cars. Emily knew Officer McBride and Officer Rowland, and it was kind of amazing to realize that this wasn't her first time in a police car. It wasn't even her first time this month!

Zack enjoyed riding in any car, and he stood up on the backseat, pressing his nose against the thick wire barricade separating them from the front seat. It was funny to imagine him as a criminal who had just been arrested.

When the police car pulled up in front of her house, her parents came rushing out, looking alarmed.

"What happened?" her mother asked. "Are you all right?"

Emily nodded. "We got a ride home, that's all." She turned towards Officer McBride. "Don't worry, I promise I won't shoplift anymore."

Officer McBride looked very stern. "Well, consider this your last warning. If it happens again, you'll be serving time."

Emily nodded solemnly, and then held up her hands. "Will baby oil take care of the rest of the fingerprint ink?"

Officer Rowland nodded. "It's worth trying. Although we usually recommend lemon juice."

Her mother had a wry smile on her face, but her father looked as though he was about to have a severe anxiety attack. He was probably already calculating how much damage an arrest record might do to her chances of getting in to a good college.

"Kurt fell off his bike," she said, so that her father would relax already. "So, I called 911."

Her father looked even more worried. "Did you and Zack do anything dangerous?"

"Well," Emily said, and pretended to think. "I pushed three numbers into my phone, and if you're not really careful, I think you can get carpal tunnel syndrome from that."

Her parents exchanged glances.

"If this is what you're like at twelve," her mother said, "I can't tell you how much I am dreading your teen years."

Emily laughed the most wicked laugh she knew how to laugh.

"I'm beginning to think that we just shouldn't let you two go outside anymore," her father said wryly.

Sometimes, these days, Emily felt that way herself!

13

Even though Emily knew he yearned for a heaping dish of meat, Zack seemed quite happy with his kibble and two small cubes of cheddar cheese. Emily always liked to put a couple of little treats into his food, and Zack always seemed to be delighted and surprised when he found them in his dish.

After dinner, Emily took him out to the backyard. Zack ambled around, sniffing at trees and bushes and rocks. She was pretty sure that he liked to look around for possible wildlife—squirrels, raccoons, rabbits, whatever—but, that he would be stunned and confused, if he actually found any.

It was fun to lie out on one of their wooden lawn chairs, and stare up at the sky. Since the weather was getting so much cooler, there weren't many mosquitos or black flies around anymore, which made it even more pleasant. Zack came over every so often, to rest his head on her arm, and look at her intensely. Then, he would wander away again.

After a while, her mother came out and sat on the chair next to hers.

"It's getting a little late," she said. "Maybe it's time to take a shower and start getting ready for bed?"

Probably, yeah, but, it was so nice out, that she was in no rush to go inside. "Okay," Emily said. "But, can I stay out here just a little longer?"

"You *may*," her mother said. "That is, if your homework is in good shape."

Emily nodded, since she had finished all of it earlier. Sometimes, she procrastinated, and ended up with a bunch of work to do after dinner. Whenever that happened, the assignments seemed harder than usual, because she would be tired. On the days when she started working on it as soon as she got home from school, she was always relieved later on that she had done it that way.

"I think you're already growing out of some of your new school clothes," her mother said. "We may need to do some shopping soon."

Emily nodded. She wasn't very particular about clothes—but, pants that were too short looked *really* goofy.

The moon had risen, and was casting beautiful, reflective light across the ocean channel. There wasn't much wind tonight, but the sound of small waves washing across the rocks was very calming.

"You seem very quiet lately," her mother said.

She did? One of the many bad things about not having a brother or sister was that she thought it made her naturally inclined to be quiet. Well, to be more accurate, not having siblings she was allowed to *know*, or even meet.

"Is everything okay at school?" her mother asked.

"Mostly, sure," Emily said. "It's a lot of new people and teachers and everything, but it feels more familiar now, and they almost all seem nice."

"*Almost?*" her mother said.

Emily shrugged. "It's a pretty big school. I *want* to like everyone, but a few of them are kind of annoying. But, I figure that some of them aren't all that crazy about me, either, so it's okay."

"Anyone in particular?" her mother asked.

When her mother sounded too casual, it was always obvious that she was probing for answers. "A couple of guys who act like they're five years old," Emily said. "And a few girls who care way too much about being popular."

Her mother nodded. "I'm afraid that's true of just about every school on the planet."

Probably. Maybe it was just human nature. "Sometimes, I wouldn't mind if there were more, you know, people of color there," Emily said. "Then, maybe, I wouldn't stick out quite as much." Which always made her feel self-conscious.

Her mother looked very alert. "Is anyone behaving badly towards you?"

Emily shook her head. If anything, they were *extra*-friendly, to show that it totally didn't matter. But, them acting like that made it seem as though it *did* matter.

"You've had a lot of changes all at once," her mother said. "And I guess I want to make sure that it doesn't all start to feel as though it's too much."

That was definitely true. It was October, and back in July, she never would have thought that she would have a dog, and that he would be able to communicate with her and read her mind, and that she would find out just enough about her birth mother to feel frustrated—and hurt.

And, yeah, she never would have predicted that she would start being able to see ghosts, too.

For starters.

"You're quiet again," her mother said.

Probably because she spent so much time thinking these days.

"In some ways, it feels as though absolutely everything has changed since you found Zack," her mother said.

Hearing his name, Zack lifted his head, wagged his tail twice, and then settled down on the grass again.

Emily sometimes forgot that she had only had Zack for a few months, since it felt as though he had always lived with them. But, her mother seemed to be trying to work her way towards a specific question, and Emily hoped that it wasn't going to be anything she didn't want to answer. "Everything's a lot better, since I got him," Emily said. "Having him really makes me happy."

"Oh, I know," her mother said. "I guess I just wish that the two of you would spend a little less time being heroic."

"We don't do it on purpose," Emily said defensively.

"No," her mother agreed. "And you've certainly helped a lot of people. But, I'm very worried that you aren't being careful enough."

Emily was going to disagree, but in the heat of the moment, her first thought was rarely about being careful. "I don't think you need to worry. Zack won't let me do anything that isn't safe."

Her mother nodded, although she didn't look convinced. "I hope not."

They sat there, listening to the waves, and the crickets, and what sounded like an owl some distance away.

"There really isn't anything you can't tell me, or your father," her mother said. "We're always here to listen, and try to help you in any way we can. So, you never have to worry about that."

Emily believed that was true, but that didn't necessarily mean that she was ready to share everything. "There are things I feel okay talking about," she said, "and there are things I would rather try to work through by myself."

"That sounds sensible enough," her mother said. "But, I hope you *do* tell us when things are bothering you, and let us help."

For a second, Emily wondered if this might be the right time to tell her about Zack, and the mind communication—and maybe even the ghost.

But, no, she really wasn't ready yet.

"What?" her mother asked.

Emily sighed. "Is being thirteen going to be even more complicated than being *twelve* seems to be?"

Her mother smiled at her. "Yes. I suspect that it probably is."

Boy, was *that* hard to imagine.

When she got upstairs, she spent a little time on the Internet, trying to find out more information about the Griswolds. The best source seemed to be the archives of all of the local newspapers, especially the *Bailey's Cove Bugle*.

She didn't know exactly when the car accident had been, but it had happened sometime around the holidays, when she was very small. So, she set up a search for approximately ten years earlier, and entered the word "Griswold."

A *lot* of references instantly came up. She looked at the first few articles, and they were about boring stuff like bond issues and property taxes. So, she changed her search to "Griswold + accident," and only about twenty articles appeared this time.

The stories were *really* sad. The Griswolds had been at a holiday party, on a snowy December night, and there were lots of photos of the crash. Even though the light wasn't very good, Emily recognized her father—looking a lot younger—in one of the pictures, working with some other people to try and free Mrs. Griswold from the battered car.

The worst part was that Mrs. Griswold had tested positive for alcohol that night! But, the articles all said that the police made statements that her blood alcohol level was way below the legal limit, and that she had probably had a glass of wine or eggnog at the party. So, she hadn't been drunk, but she had definitely had at least one drink. Mr. Griswold's blood alcohol level was a little bit higher—close to the legal limit—so, that might be why she was the one who had been driving.

Some of the quotes from people in the articles about the crash only talked about drinking and driving, which seemed pretty mean. Other quotes were mostly sympathetic, and sad. The rest of the articles included Mr. Griswold's obituary, a funeral notice, and a bunch of stories and editorials about Mrs. Griswold resigning as mayor, after the accident. Most people seemed to think that she should have stayed on as mayor, but in every single article, it said something like "Abigail Griswold could not be reached for a comment." She was described in one of the reports as being "a recluse," who was no longer involved in any town activities.

At the end of Mr. Griswold's obituary, it said that he was survived by his wife, Abigail Connolly Griswold, of Bailey's Cove, and his son, Henry Matthew Griswold, from Wiscasset, which was about twenty-five miles away.

Wait, Mrs. Griswold had a *son*? Maybe he came to visit her all the time, but Emily had never noticed. Only, if they were close, wouldn't he have shown up at the hospital when she got hurt during the hurricane? So, maybe they weren't in touch? If that was true, then it would have to be very sad and painful for Mrs. Griswold, and probably for her son, too.

Just to see what would come up, she entered "Henry Griswold" and "Wiscasset" into a couple of search engines, as well as the archives of the town newspaper in

Wiscasset. A surprising amount of information immediately popped up, including a couple of websites which listed him as a participant in some local fishing tournaments, and several newspaper articles which said that he coached Little League, and talked about his team's results in various games. She even found a website for "Griswold Hardware" on Surf Street in Wiscasset. The picture of the man smiling in front of the store was the *same* man in a picture with the Little League team.

Wow. Her parents were always saying that she needed to be careful on the Internet, and that nothing was private, even if she thought it was. She got tired of hearing about it, but, maybe they were right, after all. It certainly was easy to find out a lot of information about a person!

"If you don't get some sleep, you are never going to be able to get up tomorrow morning, Emily," her father said from the doorway.

Emily looked up from the computer. "Oh, okay. Is it late?" She glanced at the clock. It was just past eleven, which meant that it was past time for her to be in bed. So, she logged off the websites she was on, and shut her computer down.

"Were you doing anything unsafe that would make your mother and me gasp and faint?" he asked.

Emily grinned. Her father was very goofy. "Just

giving a bunch of strangers my name and address and telephone number, and stuff like that."

Her father laughed. "Okay. Nothing to worry about, then."

She had gotten a lot of lectures about Internet safety over the years from her parents *and* her teachers. So, she actually was very careful, and kept her privacy settings high, and only "friended" people whom she *knew* in real life, and that sort of thing.

Her parents still always tucked her in at night, but she had asked them to call it "saying good-night," since it sounded more grown-up. The fact that her mother turned her pillow for her, and made sure the sheets and blankets were pushed neatly under the mattress and so forth was just a coincidence.

When Emily came back into the room after brushing her teeth, her mother was, indeed, busy straightening the sheets and blankets on the bed. Zachary had already stretched out across the mattress, which was making the job a lot more complicated, of course.

"Is it true that Mrs. Griswold has a son?" Emily asked, once she had been—okay—*tucked in.*

Her parents both nodded.

"He doesn't seem to come around much," Emily said.

"No," her mother agreed. "As far as I know, they haven't spoken in years."

"Why?" Emily asked.

"I don't know," her father said. "Some sort of feud, I suppose. She isn't exactly easy to be around."

No, but it was still sad to think of members of a family not being in touch with each other.

Which was, of course, exactly like her birth family, wasn't it? Or birth mother, and unknown father, anyway.

She decided to change the subject—or, anyway, focus on the original one. "Was it before, or after, the accident?"

"After," her mother said, sounding very certain. "I remember that he and his father were always walking by with their fishing rods. They used to go over to Wigualha Creek and catch trout, I think."

Wigualha was the Abenaki word for "swan," and the Abenakis were one of the primary Native American tribes in Maine. Emily had never seen a swan anywhere near the creek, but she still liked the name.

"Do you think he was mad at her, after what happened?" Emily asked.

Her father smiled at her. "So many questions! Don't you ever get sleepy?"

Not very often, no. It *was* late, though, so she kissed each of her parents good-night, and let them turn off the lamp next to her bed. But, as she curled up, trying to find a comfortable spot that wasn't already occupied by a pet, she couldn't stop thinking about the Griswolds' son, and whether there was any way he could be reunited with his mother.

Maybe, just maybe, she had figured out how she was supposed to help Mr. Griswold!

The next afternoon, while Emily was down at the marina working on the boat with Bobby, she gave him all of the latest updates.

"Wow," he said, looking very impressed. "You're like, the Ghost Sleuth!"

Emily nodded. "Yeah. I'm going to branch out to solving crimes, and finding buried treasure and stuff, next."

Bobby looked even more impressed. "Really?"

Emily shook her head.

"Oh," Bobby said, his face falling. "Okay. But, if you do, I want to be your brave partner who always shows up in the nick of time."

Emily pointed at Zack, who was asleep in a pile of sand. "We cast that part already. Maybe you could be the wacky neighbor?"

"No," Bobby said. "That's Mrs. Griswold."

Yes, she was the much better choice for that.

"So, all this ghost stuff. Is it creeping you out?" Bobby asked.

"Not Mr. Griswold, specifically," Emily said. "Because he seems to be really sweet, and just wants to make Mrs. Griswold feel better."

Bobby shook his head. "It's hard to believe that she was married to someone nice. Like, how did he stand it?"

Good question. "I would have figured that maybe she was a lot more friendly before," Emily said, "but my parents said she pretty much always had 'a strong personality.'"

"Wow, you told your parents?" Bobby said.

Maybe she should—but, she *really* wasn't ready for that. "No," Emily said. "I asked some questions, that's all."

"Are you *going* to tell them?" he asked.

"If I can figure out a way that won't make me seem too crazy," Emily said. "Or like I'm making stuff up."

Bobby nodded, fitting a board into their boat frame, to see how it looked. "Do you think ghosts're everywhere, all the time, and we just never knew?"

That would be way creepy. "Maybe," Emily said. "Although I sort of hope not. Or that they're all happy, and don't need to interact or anything. Or that even if he sees them, Zack will just ignore most of them, unless it's some kind of total emergency, and I'll never know the difference."

Hearing his name, Zack lifted his head just long enough to wag his tail, before he went back to sleep.

"It's like a whole other world since you found Zack," Bobby said. "Everything was pretty normal before."

Yeah.

"I wonder if all of the same stuff would be happening to me, if he'd landed on the rocks near my house, instead," Bobby said.

That had never crossed her mind, but maybe Zack would have bonded with the first person he met—and it just happened to be her.

Which was kind of disappointing, because she had to admit that she wanted their relationship to be unique.

"Except, I think he was looking for you," Bobby said. "Like, it was all cosmic, and—what's the word? Destiny, maybe?"

"Yeah. But, I don't know," Emily said. She had to admit that she hoped that was true, though.

Zack must have known that they were talking about him, because he yawned, and stretched, and came over for her to pat him.

"I bet if he'd landed on our rocks," Bobby said, "he would have been friendly and all, but the first time we ran into you, it would have been like, 'Thanks, Bob, good luck, maybe I'll see you around sometime.'"

Emily laughed. "You think Zack calls you 'Bob'?"

Bobby nodded. "Absolutely. Sometimes Robert, but mostly Bob."

It was entirely possible that Zachary would do that, if he thought it would make Bobby happy.

"I should give it a try," Bobby said. He looked at Zack, obviously concentrating as hard as he could.

Zack seemed puzzled, but then, he lifted his paw.

"Wow," Emily said, impressed. "He can read your mind, too."

Bobby shook his head. "No. I was trying to get him to bring me the hammer."

Oh. So, Zack must have lifted his paw to be polite, instead of as a direct response. Emily closed her eyes, and imagined Zack picking up the screwdriver with the red handle, and carrying it over to Bobby.

Zack promptly got up and went over to the table, and looked at the three screwdrivers with a confused expression.

Were dogs color-blind? Maybe. She had never thought about that before. So, Emily mentally focused on the screwdriver on the far left of the bench, which happened to be the red one.

Zack wagged his tail, picked it up, and brought it proudly over to her.

"Take it to Bobby, instead," she said, "okay?"

Zack cocked his head to one side.

It was funny that communicating random thoughts was easy—but, speaking English could be hard. So, she sent him an image of Bobby smiling and accepting the screwdriver.

Zack turned around and brought it over to him.

"Thanks," Bobby said. "Good dog, Zack."

Zack barked with delight, accepted the biscuit Emily handed him, and went over to lie down on the sand pile to eat the dog bone in comfort.

"That was really cool, but the thing is, I wanted the hammer," Bobby said.

Emily laughed. "I know. But, I switched it to the screwdriver, so that the concept could, you know, start fresh."

"Hey, you don't have to convince *me*," Bobby said, and went over to get the hammer himself.

They worked for a few minutes in silence, and then Bobby stopped hammering.

"Hey, I've got an idea!" he said. "Let's go visit Mrs. Griswold's son!"

Emily looked at him uneasily. "Why?"

Bobby shrugged. "You're supposed to pass along the message, right? And Mr. Griswold isn't sure how to do it, seems like. So, we just go there, and—boom! Everything's cool."

That sounded too easy. But, then again, was there any good reason why it should have to be hard? "It's pretty far, though," Emily said. "It's not like we can walk over."

Bobby grinned, and took out his cell phone. "No problem." He quickly dialed, and then asked his sister Andrea if she could drive them to a hardware store. "See?" he said, when he hung up. "No problem."

Emily wasn't supposed to go places without permission, so she left a message on her mother's voice mail to let her know that Andrea was going to drive them to the hardware store—she didn't say *which* hardware store—and then, give her a ride home, and not to worry.

Andrea pulled up a few minutes later in the family car, and Bobby and Emily piled in, with Zack right behind them. The Percivals had a pickup truck, too, but Bobby's father was the only one who ever drove it.

"Why don't we just go over to Brunswick?" Andrea suggested. "Instead of all the way up there?"

"Because," Bobby said.

Andrea frowned at him suspiciously. "Are you up to something?"

Bobby nodded. "Yup. But, nothing bad."

Andrew narrowed her eyes. "For real?"

Bobby nodded again. "Absolutely. We're like, on the side of the angels."

Andrea didn't seem to be convinced, and she swiveled around to look at Emily in the backseat. "For real?"

"Yes," Emily said. In fact, it was possibly *literally* true, in this case.

Andrea shrugged. "Okay, then," she said, and put the car into drive.

Wiscasset was a totally quaint town with a very famous lobster shack, which was always crowded with tourists during the summer. But, on a quiet October afternoon, there was no traffic, and they made really good time going up there. Andrea pulled the car into a parking spot right near the store.

"Okay, you two angels," she said, sounding amused. "Zack and I will wait here, while you do whatever it is you're doing."

Emily patted Zack on the head. "Good boy. We'll be right back."

Zack looked anxious and watched her intently as she and Bobby got out of the car.

The second they walked into the hardware store, Emily knew they had made a terrible mistake. There were a fair number of people inside, shopping in different aisles, and she saw a man behind the front counter who seemed to be the right age to be the Griswolds' son and looked like the same person from the grainy newspaper photos. He was chatting with customers, and his expression was cheerful and friendly, and it was obvious that he was a very pleasant person.

"I don't think we should do this," Emily said quietly.

Bobby looked confused. "Why not? He doesn't look like he would yell at us or anything."

Maybe that was exactly why not. "Let's just go back outside," Emily said.

Bobby frowned. "I thought we were on a special mission and all. I mean, it would help Mrs. Griswold, right? And we're going to give him messages from his father and all."

Somehow, every instinct she had said that it would be the wrong thing to do. So, she shook her head. "I don't know," Emily said. "Now that we're actually here, it seems like it's not any of our business. There's helping, and then, there's just *getting in the way*."

"Are you sure?" Bobby asked.

Emily nodded. "Yeah. We would cause a bunch more problems than we would solve."

Bobby shrugged. "Okay. But, what do we tell Andrea about why we asked her to drive us all the way over here?"

That was a good question, and Emily didn't have a good answer.

Bobby's expression brightened. "Wait, I know! I have six dollars. How much do you have?"

Emily checked her pockets. "Eleven dollars, and thirty cents."

"Well, we do need some stuff for the boat," Bobby said. "We'll buy some more sandpaper, and maybe a file, and then, it won't be suspicious."

That was pretty good. It would still be a *little* suspicious, though. Emily nodded. "Okay. I guess it's good that we can support like, a local business, instead of a chain store, anyway."

Bobby grinned. "Yeah, coming from you, Andrea'll believe that."

Probably because it was exactly the sort of thing her mother would say.

So, they picked out sandpaper with two different grains, and a fine-toothed file—all of which would come in handy for the boat.

When they brought everything up to the counter, the man smiled at them.

"Find everything you need?" he asked.

They both nodded politely.

"Okay, then," he said, and started ringing up the purchases.

It was interesting, because he did look kind of like Mrs. Griswold—the same thick hair, and something about his jawline was familiar, too.

"School project?" the man asked.

Bobby shook his head. "No, we're building a boat, and we have a lot of work to do on the wood, still."

"Sailboat?" the man asked.

"No, it's going to be a skiff," Bobby said. "We're not really ready to put together a mast or a rudder or anything yet."

"Well, I'm sure it will come out great," the man said, handing them their change. "When I was a boy, my father and I built a dory together." He shook his head wistfully. "We used that boat for years."

Emily instantly wanted to ask questions about his father—but, that would be crossing a huge line, too. So, she just smiled, and kept quiet.

But, Bobby was nodding. "We might try a dory next. We're going to caulk the skiff the old-fashioned way, like my grandfather taught my father. It's going to be so cool!"

"That's the best way," the man—okay, Mr. Griswold; not that they could admit that they knew that—agreed. "More work, but you'll end up with a true classic that way."

The two of them seemed to be having a good time

doing the whole male-bonding thing, so Emily tuned out and looked around.

There were several photographs hanging on the wall behind the cash register, and Emily recognized Mrs. Griswold's house in one of them. In fact, in that photo, a younger Mrs. Griswold was standing with what looked like a younger version of the Henry Griswold they were looking at this very moment. Maybe his father had taken the photo? In another photo, Emily saw his father, Mr. Griswold, also looking much younger, holding a fishing pole, and wearing a canvas vest with lures attached to it and everything.

She wished there was something she *could* say, which would help, and put everything at peace—but, if she made a remark about the photograph, she didn't think that would accomplish much.

Since Bobby couldn't read her mind, though, he was pointing at the pictures. "Hey, is that your dad?" he asked.

Mr. Griswold turned around to look. "Sure is," he said. "He was a great guy. I miss him every day."

"I'm sorry," Bobby said. "That's really sad."

Mr. Griswold nodded, packing their purchases into a small paper bag.

"Do you have a picture of your boat?" Bobby asked.

Mr. Griswold smiled. "You know, I actually do." He

showed them an old photo on the wall of a boy about twelve years old, sitting in a boat with a man, both of them holding fishing poles.

"Wow, it floats!" Bobby said.

Mr. Griswold laughed. "Don't worry, yours will, too."

Emily leaned over to look at the picture more closely. "What's that on the bow?" she asked.

"That's technically the prow, not the bow. And that's a wooden gargoyle," Mr. Griswold said, his expression looking wistful. "I always loved gargoyles, and my mother made that for me to christen the boat."

Mrs. Griswold *made gargoyles*? The one on the boat looked sort of like a flying mermaid with the face of a lion. It was really neat. And, now that she thought about it, she actually had seen a few ornate wooden gargoyles on Mrs. Griswold's porch and in the front garden, over the years. "How did she make it?" Emily asked.

"She carved it for me," Mr. Griswold said.

That was completely and totally impossible to imagine.

"Must have taken her hours," Mr. Griswold said softly. Then, he shook his head and tucked the wallet away. "Well. Good luck with your boat, kids. If you think of it, bring me a picture of it sometime, when you're finished."

Emily and Bobby promised that they would, and waved good-bye when they left.

"What's a gargoyle?" Bobby asked, as they went outside.

"They're sculptures," Emily said. "They're usually made of stone, and they're up on buildings. You see them in New York all the time. My father told me that sometimes they're just for decoration, but that they also use them like fancy rain gutters. They're kind of scary-looking sometimes, but I like the way they look. Dragons and monsters and mythological things and all. They're supposed to keep away evil spirits, too, I think."

"And Mrs. Griswold is sitting around *carving* them?" Bobby said, and shook his head. "Weird."

Yes, it was definitely hard to picture. But, interesting.

Zack must have sensed that she was feeling very conflicted, because after she got into the car and put on her seat belt, he crawled partway onto her lap. She hugged him, half-listening while Andrea and Bobby talked about the fact that their mother's lobster rolls were *much* better than the ones sold at the famous lobster shack, and that the tourists really ought to come to Bailey's Cove for *their* lobster rolls, instead.

The road they were on was winding along right next to the ocean. As Zachary sniffed at the open window, Emily looked outside—and saw a person-sized gust of mist down by the water. It seemed to stay there just long enough for her to notice that it was there, and then, it disappeared.

Apparently, they weren't the only ones who had decided to go visiting today!

15

Emily was pretty tired when she got home, and that made it too easy to get into an argument with her parents about what she was going to do the next day after school. Bobby was heading down to Chebeague Island—he was going to be allowed to leave school early and everything—for his aunt and uncle's twenty-fifth anniversary party, and Karen had an appointment to see her orthodontist. Her friend Harriet had soccer practice, and her friend Florence had the flu, and had stayed home from school.

So, naturally, Emily and her parents spent most of dinner having the predictable discussion about whether she was old enough to stay home by herself for a few hours—and, as usual, her parents very unreasonably outvoted her.

"It's not fair," Emily said grumpily. "If I had brothers or sisters, I would *win* a lot of these votes."

Her father shook his head. "No, you wouldn't. Your mother and I would stuff the ballot box to make sure that you would still lose."

But, Emily wasn't in the mood to be amused. In fact, she felt so disagreeable that when her parents said that she could come over to the college, and wait in one of their offices, she flat-out refused. In fact, she told them that it would be totally boring, and she would *still* be alone all afternoon, and that she would hate every minute of it, and that they were extremely mean and unfair.

After all, if they were going to be difficult, *she* could be difficult, too.

"But, you come over there all the time, and it's never been a problem before," her mother said.

Emily shrugged. "Not a problem for *you* guys. You get to be all busy teaching and stuff, and I'm sitting around waiting, without even getting to play with Zack and Josephine."

Maybe her parents were tired, too, because they both sighed.

"Some of the eighth and ninth graders babysit," Emily said. "Maybe you should hire one of them to take care of me."

To her horror, for a few seconds, her father actually seemed to be giving the idea some serious consideration. So, Emily decided to change the subject—quickly.

"Maybe I should just go upstairs and read some like, financial blogs," she said. "Because I really *am* going to work on Wall Street and run a hedge fund when I grow up."

That had always been one of her best threats, since the very concept upset her parents so much.

"I think Granddad can probably help me find the toughest and most profitable firm down there, and that's where I'll go," she said, since he had spent most of his career as a financial mogul.

Her parents were fairly speechless.

The whole meal was pretty testy, and after they finished, her parents both got on their phones, scrambling around for an alternate solution. Finally, it was decided that, with Cyril's permission, Emily would go to the Mini-Mart when she got home from school and wait there. Emily wasn't crazy about the idea, but she was tired of arguing, and at least Zack could keep her company that way.

"I love the free market," Emily said.

"Well, be that as it may," her mother said—after the predictable appalled silence—"but, it's settled that you'll go to the Mini-Mart, after you get off the bus?"

"Okay," Emily said. "After I come home and get Zack first."

Her parents agreed, as though that was a *really* big concession on their part.

"And you'll call one of us, and check in, of course," her father said.

Emily nodded. But, wow, were they *always* going to be so protective? If they were, it was going to be nearly impossible to do stuff like go on dates someday.

"So, when it's time for me to go to college, will I have to commute and live at home and all?" she asked.

Her parents sighed.

"That is, if I even *go* to college," Emily said.

It was probably smart that her parents let that one pass without comment.

"I know we need to find some better solutions to the after-school situation," her mother said, "but letting you spend the afternoons at home by yourself, at this age, is not an option. Period."

"Fine, whatever," Emily said grumpily, and went into the den, partially to do homework, but mostly, to sulk.

She had noticed that when any of them had a disagreement, it made their house suddenly seem *really small*. But, instead of working on math equations, she found herself playing a few rounds of "chase the pen and try to knock it out of my hand" with Josephine, and then throwing a tennis ball back and forth across the room for Zack.

She was over by the bookcases, picking up the slobbery tennis ball, when the row of Bowdoin yearbooks on the bottom shelf caught her eye. Her parents had a collection of about twenty yearbooks, dating back to when they had first started teaching at the college.

She stared at the yearbooks for a minute and then, to Zack's disappointment, let the ball drop out of her hand and onto the floor.

There was a really good chance that her mother might be *in* one of those yearbooks.

And there probably wouldn't be that many African-American students, either. The campus was somewhat diverse, but not to the degree that she would have that much trouble picking her out, or narrowing it down, at least. Emily looked at the row of books, and then started to take down the yearbook from twelve years earlier. But, if her birth mother had left school after she got pregnant, then she was more likely to be in the one from thirteen years ago, so she pulled out that volume, too. If she wasn't a senior—and she probably wasn't, since she had transferred to another school—she wouldn't have had a formal photograph taken, but she might have been in some clubs or on a team or something.

She started with the thirteen-year-old yearbook, first. She opened it up to the first page and took her time, although it wouldn't be very hard to skim through and just look for photos of young African-American women.

"She's not in any of them," her mother said, from behind her.

Emily jumped, feeling guilty, even though she ought to have every right to find out as much as she wanted about her own birth mother. "I was just looking," she said, and kept turning pages.

Her mother nodded, and sat down across the room on the love seat.

Neither of them spoke, but after a while, Emily began to feel self-conscious. She had found the page which had a photograph of members of the college's African-American Society, and she looked at each face, hoping to see something—anything—familiar.

"Are you sure she's not in here?" Emily asked finally.

"Yes," her mother said.

She sounded so certain that it was probably true. "There's a good chance my father is in at least one of these yearbooks," Emily said.

"It's certainly possible, but he could also have been a hometown boyfriend, or someone off-campus." Her mother hesitated. "If you want to know the truth, I've looked at them myself before, wondering if I would see someone who resembled you, but I never have."

"He could be Caucasian or African-American," Emily said.

Her mother nodded. "Caucasian, I've always assumed. But, yes, either is certainly possible."

So, there was a clue in there. "You mean, my mother has pretty dark skin?" Emily asked.

Her mother seemed to weigh whether it would be okay to answer that, and then nodded.

Emily thought about that. "Do you think it could have bothered her parents, then, that I might be biracial?"

"I'm not sure," her mother said. "But, not as far as I know. They seemed like extremely good people."

Wow, it sounded like her mother knew a lot about them. "So, that means that you met them?" Emily asked.

"Just briefly," her mother said. "We really only had one conversation. Mostly, we just saw each other in passing, at the hospital. It was a very hard situation for them. Obviously, your father and I were overjoyed to be bringing you home with us, but we wanted to make the transition as easy as possible for everyone else, so we tried to be low-key." Her mother grinned suddenly. "But, wow, were we happy, once we got outside. Then, you threw up in the cab on the way to the hotel, and your father was so panicky that he wanted to turn around right away and go back and have you admitted for observation."

That was very easy to picture, since it didn't take

much to make her father nervous. Emily had always heard that her parents flew back to Portland—from somewhere or other; although she now knew that it was Atlanta—and that lots of their friends and relatives were at the house, waiting for them, and that there was a huge party. Apparently, Emily's contribution had been to have a bottle, spit up again, get her diaper changed at least twice, and then sleep the rest of the time. She had seen pictures of the party, and in most of them, she was wrapped in a green crocheted blanket that her California grandmother had made. A photo from the party of her parents holding her with huge smiles on their faces had been framed and was hanging in the front hallway.

That part of her life, at least, was real. But, everything else about who she was felt imaginary. "They're like ghosts," Emily said. A different sort of ghost, of course, but still, ghosts. "My mother. My father. All of them. I know they exist, but there's nothing *real*."

Her mother nodded unhappily.

"Do you know stuff about her?" Emily asked. "Personal stuff?"

Her mother shrugged a tiny affirmative shrug.

"But, you're not going to tell me," Emily said.

Her mother sighed. "You know that my primary

loyalty is to you, but I gave her my word, all of those years ago, and I need to abide by that."

Integrity was a really good thing—except when it wasn't.

What she really wanted was a detail of some kind— like "Your mother was a terrific soccer player" or "She was a whiz at chemistry" or that she loved poetry or anything specific like that.

The room was quiet.

Zack was making dog mumbles in his sleep, and Emily patted him gently, to soothe whatever dream he was having.

"She sang," her mother said.

Emily looked up, startled.

"She was in an a capella group, on campus," her mother said. "I never got a chance to hear her myself, but I'm told by people who did that she has an absolutely gorgeous voice."

Wow. "I can barely sing at all," Emily said. "Or, anyway, not really on key."

Her mother shrugged. "Just one of those things, I guess."

Maybe her birth father had been tone-deaf. But, she finally knew something true, and something *real*, about her past.

"Well," her mother said. "It's a start, right?"

Yes, it definitely was.

During study hall the next day, she told Karen, and her friends Harriet and Florence, about the tiny little nugget of information she had learned about her birth mother. Then, because it was too hard to keep so many secrets—especially from her friends—she told them about everything else that had been going on lately, too, since she could now see *ghosts*, on top of everything else.

"Zack is amazing," Florence said. "I'm not even sure if Tabitha knows her name."

Emily laughed, because Florence's dog, who was a flaky little spaniel mix, *did* always seem to have trouble understanding even the most basic things, like "Sit" or "Come."

"So, okay, if ghosts are real," Harriet said, "does that mean that vampires are real, too?"

"No," Emily said, with great authority. "Werewolves and leprechauns are real, but vampires and sprites and monsters are all fake."

Her friends looked very impressed.

"Wow," Florence said. "You know that for sure?"

Emily was tempted to play it out, and keep teasing

them, but decided that it might be mean. "No," she said. "I was just kidding around."

Harriet thought about that. "So, vampires *could* be real."

Karen shook her head. "I hope not. My mother says that most of the stuff about vampires totally objectifies women and everything."

Which was one reason why Emily's mother and Karen's mother got along.

"What about female vampires?" Harriet asked logically.

Karen shrugged. "I don't know, I'll have to ask her. Maybe they're okay?"

This was definitely a dumb conversation, and Emily laughed. "If vampires were real, wouldn't they *all* be bad, one way or another? Like, maybe not sexist and stuff, but just plain old *evil*?"

Florence pretended to look stern. "That's very vampirist of you."

"Totally politically incorrect," Karen agreed.

Somewhere, there probably *was* a group devoted to protecting the reputations of vampires. "If vampires really existed, we'd have a bunch of people yelling at each other on television all the time about whether they're good, or bad, and how anyone who disagrees with them is even *more* bad," she said. As a political scientist, her mother was very big on the concept that disagreeing with an idea didn't mean that you had to dislike the *person* who happened to suggest it.

Harriet looked around uneasily. "Well, I hope that Mr. Griswold is the *only* ghost around, and that none of those other things are real. Because if they are real, I'm going to have about seven hundred nightmares tonight."

If it turned out that there were a whole bunch of werewolves and vampires and monsters hanging around on Earth, looking for trouble, Emily was going to have nightmares, too.

"Are you girls studying?" their teacher asked, from the front of the room.

All four of them nodded innocently, and focused down on their books—none of which were even open.

Florence flipped to the third chapter in their Spanish book, to start doing her homework. "One thing's for sure," she whispered. "Your life is really *exciting* these days, Emily."

Boy, was it ever!

Emily took the bus home after school, and went straight into the Mini-Mart to let Cyril know that she was going home to get Zack first, and would bring him right back with her.

And, mostly, that was exactly what she did. She took the time to put on a fleece sweatshirt, since the air was definitely starting to feel like autumn. She also patted Josephine for a little while, changed the water in her dish, and fed her.

Then, since she was getting nonstop images of Zack's dish *overflowing* with food, she fed him, too. Usually, he only had a couple of dog biscuits when she got home from school, and didn't eat supper until about six, but apparently, he was extra-hungry today.

Of course, once they got down to the Mini-Mart, Cyril was bound to give Zack all sorts of treats, but Emily assumed that he would have no trouble gobbling them down.

Zack barked happily, so she assumed that he knew

precisely what she was thinking—and liked the idea. He finished his food, and then went out to stand by the back door.

"Okay," she said to Josephine, giving her one last pat on the head. "Be a good girl."

In return, she got a flash of a blur of fur racing through every room in the house, leaving behind a path of total destruction. Shredded sofa cushions and pillows, broken glasses and dishes, silverware strewn across the kitchen floor, books knocked off every shelf of *every* bookcase, framed photos and paintings falling off the walls—the house was pretty much *trashed*.

Then, she could have sworn she heard—or, no, *sensed*—a really high-pitched sound that was apparently cat laughter. Cat *cackling*, actually.

Reading Josephine's mind was always a little bit unsettling.

Zack must have also tuned in, because he barked very, very sharply—and Emily was pretty sure she sensed more gales of cat laughter.

"Maybe you could just like, take a nice nap on the windowsill in the sun," Emily said.

All she got back was a sound that might be a cat snicker.

Before going outside, Emily checked all of the windows, to make sure that they were closed. Since Josephine was obviously feeling mischievous today, Emily wouldn't put it past her to sneak out and follow them. Granted, Josephine already seemed to be asleep on the couch—but, she might be faking it.

The leaves were starting to turn, and fall was definitely coming. Emily liked fall, for lots of reasons, including the fact that the air smelled extra-clean and sharp. But, it had started raining while she was in the house, and so, she and Zack walked along more quickly than they would have otherwise.

Emily had assumed that she would sit outside at the picnic table, and listen to people's stories for a couple of hours while she was waiting for her father to come and pick her up. But, since it was raining even harder now, that idea seemed much less appealing.

Before opening the front door of the store, Emily pictured Zack shaking energetically, so that he would be a little less wet when they went inside—and he cooperatively did just that. Cyril was waiting for them with an old beach towel, and Emily used it to dry Zack off even more, making sure to spend extra time on his paws, in case someone came in whom he really liked and felt like jumping up to greet.

When she was finished, she hung the towel up neatly on a small coatrack, which was right next to the entrance.

Cyril had set up a card table with a new sketch pad, some pens and colored pencils, a small carton of cold orange juice, a wooden bowl with pretzels, and a dish of M&M's. Seeing all of that made her feel as though maybe she wasn't imposing as much as she had been afraid she might be, since it looked as though he *liked* the idea of babysitting for an afternoon.

So, she sat down, and drew quietly, and sipped juice. Zack slept under the table, sprawled across her feet—which made her sneakers feel even more wet, but she didn't mind at all.

Mostly, she drew the activity in the store—customers coming in and out, people standing in small clumps to chat briefly, Mr. Washburn—who regularly hung out at the store—lounging by the ice cream freezer as he read the latest edition of the *Bailey's Cove Bugle*, and Cyril hustling around to locate obscure items on various shelves, and ringing up people's purchases, while he made a near-constant stream of offbeat comments and observations. Every so often, he would pause to check on her, and she would assure him that she was fine and ask if he needed any help, and he would say, no, no, it's under control.

The steady stream of customers slowed down as the rain outside came down harder.

"What are you drawing?" Cyril asked, after he

wiped down various display cases, and straightened a few shelves.

Emily couldn't help feeling shy. She didn't even always show her parents her drawings, especially if they didn't come out very well. "Nothing special. Just, you know, *stuff.*"

"Is it okay if I look?" he asked.

She was afraid that he wouldn't like them, but she handed the sketchbook to him. He sat down across the table from her, and took his time going through the pad, paying close attention to each and every sketch.

"These are *very* good, Emily," he said.

Well, grown-ups always said things like that, to be nice. She shrugged self-consciously. "Thank you. I was just practicing."

"They're absolutely *spiffy*," he said. "Would it be all right if I keep this one?"

She leaned over and saw that he had picked out a sketch she had done of him standing behind the cash register, gesturing with both hands and looking as though he was in the middle of a long and *opinionated* conversation. "Sure," she said, genuinely surprised. "You, um, like it?"

He nodded, and went down one of the aisles to poke through a shelf. He returned with a new black picture frame.

"I'm going to hang it right up," he said, "so that everyone will be able to see it, but I want you to sign it, first."

Oh, dear. "But, it's not finished," she said uncomfortably. "There's a lot more I should do, to make it better."

He shook his head. "It's perfect, just the way it is."

She felt shy, but carefully wrote her name and the date on the bottom right-hand corner of the page.

"There," he said, looking pleased. "Now, when you're famous someday, I'll already own one of your early works, and everyone will be jealous."

Not that Emily wanted to be famous, particularly, but the idea of being a professional artist was definitely appealing.

Since she was curious, she decided to ask a sort of personal question. "You like children, sir?" she said. "I mean, you know, except for Bobby."

"*Bobby*," Cyril said, and shook his head. "I'm afraid he's a shifty-eyed, squinty little punk."

Right. Whatever. "Okay, but other than that, you like children?" Emily asked.

Cyril nodded. "My wife and I wanted children more than I can tell you. But then, she got sick, and—" His eyes looked distant and sad. "Well. Things don't always work out the way you hope they will."

She had never met Cyril's wife, who had died at least

twenty years ago, but people in town always said really complimentary things about her. "I've heard she was a really great person," Emily said, tentatively.

Cyril nodded. "You would have liked her. And pretty as a picture? You bet! I never stopped being thankful that she was willing to marry me." He sighed, and took out his wallet, to look at a photograph, which he showed her.

"Wow. She was beautiful," Emily said. And she really *was*. In the photo, she looked like a model.

"I'll never stop missing her," Cyril said, putting his wallet away. "And it was a great loss for both of us, that we weren't able to have a child. My friend Sam used to drag me along when he took his son fishing, or to ballgames, or I'd go over to the house to have supper, and—well, I enjoyed every minute."

Sam. Emily sat up straight. "You mean, Mr. Griswold?"

Cyril nodded, looking sad again. "Not a day goes by that I don't miss him, too." He glanced over. "You know about what happened?"

Boy, did she ever. Emily nodded back.

"Terrible loss," Cyril said. "I'll never get over that one, either."

Emily nodded, letting a respectful silence pass. "So, you used to be friends with Mrs. Griswold?" she asked.

Cyril nodded. "You bet. Abigail was always a hand-ful, but she was so full of energy, I figured she'd be governor someday." He grinned. "Or maybe take over a small country somewhere."

That had to be a joke, so Emily laughed.

"But, after it happened, she pushed *everyone* away," he said. "Even Hank, their son. And, after a while—well, people make their choices. Me, I didn't have any patience for it."

"Do you think the accident was her fault?" Emily asked.

Cyril shook his head. "People say some right foolish things about that night, but, no. There's a reason they call them *accidents*."

For some reason, that made Emily think of her birth mother—who sang with a glorious voice. She had gotten pregnant *by accident*, and maybe, after that, she had just tried to make the best decisions possible. Maybe she had made some mistakes—but, maybe that was okay.

Maybe.

Maybe not.

Cyril looked at her curiously. "What?"

"I was just thinking," Emily said. Then, she changed the subject. "Are you always going to be mad at Bobby?"

Cyril frowned. "The criminal strain runs deep in his blood."

Sometimes, Emily thought that his whole attitude towards Bobby—and Bobby's entire family—was a complete put-on, but she wasn't always sure. "I think he's reformed," she said. "Left his, you know, *bad ways* in the past. Plus, of course, he's my friend, and so, it really matters to me."

Cyril moved his jaw. "Tell you what," he said, after a long pause. "I'll move the line he has to stand behind closer to the store."

That was so ridiculous that Emily laughed.

Cyril laughed, too. "I can probably do better than that, can't I?"

Without a doubt. Emily tried to think of a better compromise. "What if you take away the line completely," she said, "as long as he stops in front of the door every time he comes inside, and does five push-ups?" Since Cyril was a proud veteran, she figured that might appeal to him.

Cyril mulled that over. "All right. Make it ten push-ups, *every single time*, and we have a deal."

Could Bobby do ten push-ups? Probably. If not, she would just let him know that he should start practicing. "Sounds good to me," she said.

Her father showed up at the store around five thirty, and thanked Cyril several times.

"My pleasure," Cyril said. "Emily and Zack are good company. They're welcome here anytime at all."

"Thank you," Emily said shyly. "It was very nice of you to let us spend the afternoon with you."

"Happy to do it," Cyril said, and then winked at her. "Even if you *are* friends with a snaggle-toothed punk."

She would have to email Bobby as soon as she got home, and let him know that he had better start working on his push-ups.

"Did you have a good time?" her father asked, as they got into the car.

She had, but she was determined not to admit it. "It was okay," she said. "Even though I am *completely* old enough to stay home by myself."

Her father smiled. "Yes, I think I remember you mentioning that at least once before."

Or even a few thousand times.

"You know, one of these days, we'll actually break down, and start letting you come home alone after school," he said, checking both ways before turning out onto the road. "What will you complain bitterly about then?"

That was a good question. "I don't know," Emily said. "I guess I'll think of something. Do you have any ideas?"

Her father shrugged. "How much time to spend on

your homework, curfews, dating, whether you can bor-row the car *again*, or maybe how much we embarrass you in public?"

Emily nodded. "Those are all pretty good. I'll have to be sure and pick one of those."

"Good. Something to look forward to!" her father said cheerfully.

Yes, she could hardly wait herself.

New and interesting family arguments.

Yay!

Before they sat down to dinner that night, her mother fixed an extra plate, and covered it carefully with foil.

"What's that?" Emily asked.

Her mother shrugged. "I can't help worrying about Mrs. Griswold. She's so stubborn, that she may not be eating properly. So, let me just run this down there, before we eat."

"Want me to take it?" Emily asked.

Her mother hesitated, then nodded. "Sure. Why not? But, don't be gone too long, okay?"

So, Emily snapped on Zachary's leash, while her mother packed the hot plate and a package of homemade brownies into a small picnic basket.

"Can you manage that without any trouble?" her mother asked.

Emily hefted the basket experimentally. "Sure. No problem."

So, she and Zack walked down to Mrs. Griswold's house, and Emily knocked on the door. It took a long time, but finally, Mrs. Griswold opened it, balancing on her walker. She looked frail, and tired—and *lonely*.

"Yes?" she asked, sounding just as annoyed as she always did. "What do you want, Emily?"

Emily held out the basket. "My mother made way too much, and she thought you might like some supper?"

"Oh." Mrs. Griswold looked surprised, and maybe slightly embarrassed. "Yes. I see. Well, that was very thoughtful of her. I'm perfectly fine, though."

Emily bit her lip, not sure what she was supposed to do. "Does that mean you want me to take it back home?"

Mrs. Griswold hesitated. "No, I—thank you. Perhaps, you could just set it on the table?"

Emily felt shy about going into the house, but Zack had already bounced inside and jumped up onto the couch.

"No, Zack!" Emily said quickly. "Down, boy!"

He wagged his tail and looked at her with his bright brown eyes, staying right where he was.

Mrs. Griswold's mouth twitched to one side, as though she had thought about smiling. "I see that his obedience training has been very successful."

Not at the moment, that was for sure. "*Down*, Zack," Emily said more firmly.

She knew he wanted to stay right where he was, but he climbed down, managing to knock over two books, a stack of magazines, and the television remote on the way. Emily quickly bent down and picked everything up.

"Don't bother yourself, child," Mrs. Griswold said. "It's not a big deal."

Emily arranged everything back on the coffee table, including the picnic basket from her mother. "He's very clumsy sometimes," Emily said. "I don't think he knows how big he is." In fact, sometimes, she suspected that he thought he was only about the size of a cat!

"No harm," Mrs. Griswold said, making her way painfully towards the couch, on her walker. "Would you mind letting yourself out? And please, thank your mother for her kindness."

It made Emily sad to think of Mrs. Griswold spending the evening all by herself, and she stood there for a minute, not wanting to leave quite yet.

"Well, what is it?" Mrs. Griswold asked impatiently. "I simply can't abide dithering. Just spit it out."

Could she? *Should* she?

Zack nudged her hand, comfortingly, and she patted him on the head, trying to get her nerve up.

It had been years; there was no reason that she had to bring the subject up *today*. In fact, there was really no reason that she *ever* had to mention it. Because it really wasn't any of her business, and she hadn't exactly asked to encounter a ghost, or anything like that.

"It wasn't your fault," Emily said.

Mrs. Griswold shrugged that off. "I'll heal. It was my own choice not to evacuate to the shelter."

If Mrs. Griswold thought she was only talking about the hurricane, that gave her a graceful way out. She could nod, and agree—and *leave*.

But, Zack was leaning heavily against her legs, as though he was trying to push her forward. And it was hard to ignore a large furry conscience.

Emily swallowed. "The accident," she said. "It wasn't your fault."

Mrs. Griswold's expression darkened. "That's not something I discuss. Ever. And you're a child; what do *you* know about it?"

A lot more than Mrs. Griswold thought she did.

"That's why they call them *accidents*," Emily said. "If not, they would call them 'on purposes' or something. I'm supposed to—" No, wait, that part was a secret, and she wasn't supposed to tell Mrs. Griswold about it. "I mean, it was a bad accident. A *terrible* accident. But, no one blames you. They really don't."

Mrs. Griswold laughed harshly. "Of course people blame me. *I* blame me." She hoisted herself up onto her walker. "Now, I would like you to leave immediately, please. I don't need anyone—especially a youngster who wasn't even there—telling me how I'm supposed to feel."

Fine. Emily would be *glad* to leave—and never, ever come back.

"Am I your volunteer project or something?" Mrs. Griswold demanded. "Are you going to get public service credits for being nice to the old lady down the street?"

Wow, she really was mean! "Don't worry," Emily said quietly. "I'm leaving now. I'm not going to bother you again."

Zack still seemed to want to stay, but she gave his leash a quick tug, and he reluctantly followed her towards the front door.

Then—for no clear reason—something weird popped into her head, and she found herself saying it aloud.

"My little buttercup has the sweetest smile," she said.

Mrs. Griswold's head snapped around. "What?!"

Emily had no idea—and was kind of freaked out by having said something that made absolutely no sense. But, she had an intense urge to do it again. "Dear little buttercup, won't you stay awhile," she said, and blinked.

Zack wagged his tail and did something with his front paws that almost looked like *dancing*.

Mrs. Griswold had gone completely pale, and she looked as though she was trembling. "What made you say that?"

Since she had no idea, Emily just shrugged defensively.

"You need to go now," Mrs. Griswold said, her voice shaking.

Emily nodded, feeling a little dazed, and confused—and scared.

"Now!" Mrs. Griswold yelled. "Get out of here!"

Emily nodded—and *ran*!

It was a huge relief to get outside in the fresh air—and *away* from Mrs. Griswold. Emily stopped at the edge of the porch to catch her breath, her heart pounding so loudly that she couldn't hear anything else.

Okay, she had said something unexpected. Something that didn't make sense. Something that hadn't come out of her mind—*or* Zack's. It wasn't the end of the world, though. She would just go home, and tell her parents she didn't feel well—because, right now, she *didn't*. They would bundle her off to bed, bring her supper on a tray, and everything would be okay again.

She was feeling dizzy, so she took a few deep breaths to try and calm down. Zack was standing very close to her, and she leaned on him as she made her way down the steps.

There was a black-and-white Border collie she had never seen before playing gaily in the front yard, and Emily stared at it for a second.

Zack yanked the leash out of her hand and ran over to greet the dog. The two dogs wagged their tails, and then began galloping around wildly in one of those "only dogs know the rules" games.

As Emily walked closer, she saw that the Border collie looked sort of—*shimmery*. That might not be a word, but the dog had what looked like a slight golden glow.

Which gave her the sinking sensation that this might be yet another *ghost*.

Great.

Just great.

Not that Zack seemed to mind at all, as he raced back and forth, and jumped, and dodged, and rolled on the ground, playing happily.

"They look like they're having fun," a voice next to her said—and Emily jumped about a foot. Maybe even *two* feet.

Okay. It was only Mr. Griswold. But, still. Emily took another deep breath, and wiped her sleeve across her face, since it felt as though she was perspiring. "Is that dog Marigold?" she asked.

Mr. Griswold nodded proudly. "Yes, that's my girl. Isn't she a beauty?"

No question—she was a really neat-looking dog. "Why is she here?" Emily asked. More to the point, why could Emily *see* her?

Mr. Griswold shrugged. "I think she visits a lot. I can't say for certain, though."

Okay. "Why is she all like, glow-y?" Emily asked.

Mr. Griswold shrugged again. "There are many answers I do not have."

Right. Well, what else was new? "I don't want to be rude, sir," Emily said, "but am I *always* going to see a bunch of ghosts now? Because I would kind of rather not have it be a regular thing, you know?"

Mr. Griswold smiled at her. "You and your Zachary have a special gift. You're going to be able to help people in so many different ways."

It was nice to be able to help, but that certainly wasn't what she wanted to hear. "So, I *am* going to see ghosts all the time?" she said.

"I think not," he answered. "You will help in various ways, at various times. You will have many choices."

Well, she hadn't exactly helped Mrs. Griswold, had she? In fact, as far as she could tell, all she had managed to do was scare the daylights out of her. "It doesn't always work," she said. "Even when I try."

"My Abby wasn't ready to talk about it?" he said.

That was an understatement.

"She can be stubborn," he said. "It's just her way."

Another understatement. Emily looked at him nervously. "I said some weird stuff about buttercups. It didn't make any sense at all. Did you make me do that?"

He shook his head. "I was thinking of things Abigail would associate only with me—and you must have sensed that."

She would *way* rather not be able to read a ghost's mind. In fact, all of this was so confusing, that she decided to sit down on the grass for a minute. But, it didn't help that Zack was joyfully chasing a *ghost* dog back and forth right in front of her.

Mr. Griswold sat down next to her, although he seemed to hover slightly above the actual ground. "As you learn and experience more," he said, "it will be easier for you to control your gifts. You will be able to be open to things you want to sense, but block the ones which trouble you."

Good. The sooner, the better. "Why didn't you just come inside and talk to her directly?" Emily asked. "Wouldn't that have been easier?"

Mr. Griswold looked horrified. "We must not cause pain, because of the task. My beloved would not be ready for me to appear like that."

Ghosts had a lot of rules. "Does she have to invite you in?" Emily asked. "Like, you know, vampires?"

Mr. Griswold looked confused. "I do not understand that."

Well, he was probably pretty far behind on his pop

culture, what with being dead and all. And—vampires weren't real.

As far as she knew.

Marigold came gamboling over, and Emily reached down to pat her—because that was what you did with dogs. The fur felt—normal. Then, she pulled her hand away. "Her fur feels regular. I mean, like Zack's."

Mr. Griswold nodded. "Yes, she is able to appear that way. She is very advanced."

Apparently so. "What am I supposed to do now?" Emily asked.

Mr. Griswold smiled a sweet smile at her. "Go home. Do not let your parents worry about you. We worry so much about the ones we love."

Emily nodded, and slowly got up. "Okay. But, what if—" She stopped, and looked around at the yard.

Somehow, it wasn't surprising that Mr. Griswold and Marigold had disappeared into thin air.

Emily put her hands on her hips, not sure whether to be frustrated—or laugh. "I really wish you could talk," she said to Zack. "Because this ghost stuff is really wacky, you know?"

As far as she could tell, Zachary was just happy, and hungry.

So, they hustled home, where her parents were waiting.

"Goodness, what took so long?" her mother asked.

Emily couldn't even think of where to begin. "Mrs. Griswold is a complicated person," she said finally.

"Can't argue with that," her mother said.

No, it was something they could all pretty much take for granted, wasn't it.

The telephone rang while they were packing away the leftovers and cleaning up the kitchen. Her mother answered it, and looked very surprised.

"Hello, Abigail," she said. "Is everything all right?"

Abigail? Emily tensed, wondering if Mrs. Griswold was calling to complain, or to tell her parents that their daughter was a lunatic who talked about buttercups.

Her mother listened, and then shook her head. "No, I'm afraid that's not possible. It's much too late on a school night, and she still has homework to do. Is there something I can do to help you?" She listened some more. "Oh. Well, I don't know, let me check." She held her hand over the receiver. "Emily, Mrs. Griswold would like you and Zack to come over for tea tomorrow afternoon. Is that okay?"

What? "Um, I don't drink tea," Emily said, because

she was so surprised that she couldn't think of any other response.

, Her mother smiled. "Well, I'm sure she will be able to give you a glass of juice or milk, instead." She reached for a piece of paper with her free hand, quickly wrote something on it, and held it up.

The note on the paper said *I can make an excuse for you, if you don't want to go.*

Emily *didn't* want to go, but she was too curious to turn the invitation down. "What time am I supposed to be there?" she asked.

Her mother held up five fingers, and Emily nodded.

"Yes, she'll be there at five," her mother said into the telephone. "Is there anything you would like her to bring you? And should I come along?" She listened. "No? I see. All right, then. Good night." She hung up the telephone and looked at Emily quizzically. "Is there something your father and I should know here?"

Was this maybe, finally, the right time to tell them? "Zack is, um, special," Emily said.

Her parents nodded.

Hearing his name, Zack got up and stood next to her, and she rested her hand on his broad shoulders.

"*Really* special," Emily said.

Her parents nodded again.

Did they maybe already know that she and Zack read each other's minds, and had just never said anything? "So, since we're kind of, um, connected," Emily said, "because he likes Mrs. Griswold, I guess I like her, too."

"That makes sense," her father said. "But, I'll certainly be curious to see how it goes tomorrow."

Emily looked at him, honestly not sure whether he knew what she meant and wasn't at all surprised—or whether he had completely missed what she was trying to say.

"Me, too," her mother said, and glanced up at the clock. "Oh, gosh, look at the time. How much homework do you have left?"

Okay, they didn't know. She didn't *think* so, anyway.

Or, did they?

She truly had no idea.

"Emily?" her mother prompted her.

Did they know, and just took it for granted, and didn't need explanations? "Uh, some Spanish and some social studies," Emily said.

Her mother nodded. "All right. Can we help you with it?"

"No, I'm fine, thanks," Emily said.

They didn't know.

As far as she could tell.

Maybe.

When Bobby found out that she was going to have tea with Mrs. Griswold, he was eager to join her. Emily didn't think that was such a great idea, under the circumstances, and he admitted that he pretty much despised tea—which made her laugh, since that was one of her big worries, too.

Her mother picked her up at school, and gave Bobby a ride home, too.

"Call me after," he whispered, before he got out of the car. "Tell me everything!"

Emily nodded.

Her mother seemed jittery, but just fixed her a snack of sliced apples and yoghurt, as though it was a perfectly typical afternoon.

"What if this spoils my tea?" Emily asked.

Her mother checked her expression to make sure she was kidding, and then smiled. "I'm sure you'll think of something."

After finishing her snack, Emily did the reading assignment for language arts, and then spent a few minutes brushing Zack. His fur was glossy and thick, and she thought he looked very handsome, indeed.

Just before she was going to leave, her father got home.

"Remember, send us a signal, if you need help," he said. "One if by land, two if by sea."

Right. Emily laughed, and snapped Zachary's leash onto his collar.

"Cell phone?" her mother asked.

Emily nodded, and patted the pocket of her hoodie.

It was a fairly chilly day, with the sun bright in the autumn sky, and no clouds anywhere. Zack was in a good mood, and stopped to sniff a rock, and a telephone pole, and a blueberry bush, on the way.

Mrs. Griswold was sitting on the new wicker love-seat on her porch—since the old one had been smashed in the hurricane—waiting for them. Emily started up the front steps, but then stopped, when she realized that Mrs. Griswold was holding a cigarette.

Emily stared at her. "Wait. You smoke *cigarettes*?"

"No," Mrs. Griswold said, and then looked down at her hand. "Well, not for many, many years. I found half a pack in a junk drawer in the kitchen." She frowned. "It's actually pretty stale. I could have done without it."

Emily hung back. "I'm sorry, but I'm not allowed to be anywhere near secondhand smoke."

Mrs. Griswold laughed. "Your parents don't miss a trick, do they?" She sighed, took one last puff on the cigarette, and then stubbed it out in the ashtray on the end table. Then, she picked up a magazine and waved it rapidly back and forth to blow the smoke away. "All right. The coast is clear."

Emily nodded and walked up onto the porch, with Zack trailing along behind her. But, the coast—smoke—must not have been *quite* clear, because Zack sneezed and then looked at Mrs. Griswold reproachfully.

"My goodness," Mrs. Griswold said wryly. "Even the dog is giving me a lecture."

With good reason!

Emily sat down in a wicker rocking chair, and Zack sat next to her on the porch floor, his posture very straight.

"Well," Mrs. Griswold said, and poured each of them a cup of tea.

"Thank you," Emily said, and put *a lot* of sugar in her cup.

There was also a plate of cookies on the table, and Emily helped herself to one. Zack looked so mournful when he saw her bite into it, that she broke off a piece and handed it to him.

She and Mrs. Griswold sipped their tea. Emily didn't like it much, but the sugar helped.

"You're attuned to that dog in some unusual way," Mrs. Griswold said. "Although I can't quite put my finger on it."

Again, with the "that dog" stuff. She must have looked annoyed, because Mrs. Griswold chuckled.

"Right," she said. "I meant to say 'Zachary.'"

Okay. That was much better. "Thank you," Emily said. "He really prefers that, although he also likes me to call him 'Zack.'"

Mrs. Griswold nodded. "Yes, I'm sure he does. But, my question is, how do you *know* that?"

Wouldn't it be strange if Mrs. Griswold, of all people, was the first grown-up to figure it out? "I was guessing?" Emily said.

Mrs. Griswold frowned at her. "Don't be one of those silly girls who makes everything she says sound like a question, even when it isn't. It shows a lack of confidence."

Well, she was only *twelve*. Sometimes, she didn't necessarily *feel* confident.

Like, for example, in this particular situation.

"He's my dog," Emily said, making sure that her voice sounded calm and certain. "We spend a lot of time together, so I can probably sense a few things."

Mrs. Griswold shook her head. "It's more than that—I've watched the two of you together many times.

You don't always speak to him, but he instantly responds, anyway. I've found it quite uncanny."

Oops. She must have slipped up a few times, because when she was in front of people, she tried to make a point of saying things aloud, to make it seem as though Zack was just really well-trained. "He's my dog," Emily said, again. "Weren't you like, in tune with *your* dog?"

Mrs. Griswold raised her eyebrows. "Dog?"

"You know, Marigold," Emily said. "Your Border collie."

Now, Mrs. Griswold looked startled. "How could you possibly know about *Marigold*? That was years ago."

Double oops. "Um, my parents told me you had a dog," Emily said.

But, it was clear that Mrs. Griswold wasn't buying that. "Have you been talking to my son?" she asked.

Not the question she had been expecting. Emily shook her head, but that wasn't quite the truth. "I was in his store for a few minutes," she said. "But it felt like it wasn't any of my business, so I didn't say anything. Bobby and I just bought sandpaper to use on the boat and then, we left." She glanced at Mrs. Griswold. "Did you know he only lives over in Wiscasset?"

"We may not be in touch," Mrs. Griswold said stiffly, "but obviously, I know where he *lives*."

Okay. Whatever.

Mrs. Griswold picked up her tea, avoiding Emily's eyes. "How—did he look?"

"Your son?" Emily asked, just to be sure.

Mrs. Griswold nodded. "His name's Hank."

"He seemed, you know, fine," Emily said. "Bobby said we were building a boat, and he told us about a boat that he and, um, Mr. Griswold built. He had a picture and everything."

Mrs. Griswold nodded a very stiff nod.

Then, Emily noticed that there was a gargoyle in the shape of an eagle perched up in the eaves of the porch, and another wooden gargoyle attached to the corner of the porch railing. That one was a wolf—or maybe a dog?—with wings. "Did you make those gargoyles?" she asked, pointing.

Mrs. Griswold moved her jaw. "Yes, I did," she said.

"They're really great," Emily said. "How did you do it?"

Mrs. Griswold smiled wryly. "I chiseled away all of the wood that didn't belong there."

What a cool way of thinking about art! Drawing was different—it was more about adding everything that *did* belong on the page.

"Did Hank tell you about the movie?" Mrs. Griswold asked.

Emily looked at her blankly.

"My little buttercup has the sweetest smile," Mrs. Griswold said.

Oh. Emily shook her head. "No. I mean, we were only in there for a minute, and—no."

"But, there's no other way you could have found out about that," Mrs. Griswold said. "It was one of my husband's favorites, and—" She stopped. "It was a private joke," she said—whispered, really. "I doubt Hank ever even knew about it."

If Emily had to make a guess, that was probably true. Zack came over and rested his head on her lap, and she automatically rubbed the back of his ears, which was his favorite place to be patted.

"I don't believe any of that beyond-the-grave foolishness," Mrs. Griswold said, her voice too loud. "It's just wishful thinking."

Emily shrugged, instead of saying anything.

"But, you've been in contact with Sam somehow," Mrs. Griswold went on. "That's the only other explanation."

Yes.

But, should she admit it?

Mrs. Griswold leaned forward. "Please tell me. It means a great deal to me."

It was scary to start, because it was going to sound so unbelievable. But, Emily took a deep breath. "We were watching the kayak races and Zack went over to a man who was standing near the bridge," she said. "I thought he was just a regular person, so I was talking to him. Zack was being really friendly, so I figured he must be okay."

Mrs. Griswold looked dubious—and uneasy, but she nodded.

"It all seemed kind of bizarre, when I thought about it," Emily said. "So, I went back a couple of days later. And we saw him again, and then, it all started to make sense." Was that the right word? "Well, not 'sense,' necessarily, but it was, you know, *logical*."

"Is he all right?" Mrs. Griswold asked, her expression very intense.

Emily nodded. "Oh, yeah, definitely. He just says he has like, a task, and I was thinking, *whoa*, he's been here for all those years? But, he said that time is different for him, and it didn't feel that way. I don't know how it works, though. He couldn't really explain it."

She had the sense that Mrs. Griswold wanted to run into the house to get away from this conversation—and if she hadn't been stuck on a walker these days, maybe she would have.

"Um, we don't have to talk about this," Emily said. "I know it's all really strange, and—"

Mrs. Griswold brushed that aside with an abrupt

move of her hand. "Is he haunting the area, because he's tormented?"

Emily shook her head. "He's haunting the area because *you're* tormented," she said quietly.

Neither of them spoke for a minute, and Emily wasn't sure whether the silence was awkward, or just thoughtful.

"He needs to be sure you're okay, and know that the accident wasn't your fault," she said. "And that you're like, letting the world back in, and all."

"Sam uses 'like' and 'and all' and such now?" Mrs. Griswold asked.

Emily felt her face get hot. "No, I was just, you know, paraphrasing, and—"

"Kidding," Mrs. Griswold said.

Right. Okay. "My parents don't like it when I speak that way," Emily said. "But, I always forget, and do it, anyway."

Mrs. Griswold nodded, smiling slightly. Then, she looked more serious. "Does he—come into the house?"

Emily shook her head. "No. He was definite about that. If he comes near here, I don't think he ever leaves the road out there. He said he doesn't want to do anything that causes pain."

"He wouldn't," Mrs. Griswold said, her eyes looking very bright. "He was a gentleman, and a gentle man."

It certainly seemed that way.

Mrs. Griswold didn't say anything for a couple of minutes, and Emily looked out at the front yard, where new grass was starting to grow in the spot where the big tree had been before the hurricane blew it down.

"I don't believe any of this for a minute, of course," Mrs. Griswold said, sounding less certain than that sentence maybe sounded. "I recognize that you're a kind child, and want to help a lonely old lady, but making up fanciful stories really doesn't—"

Zack jumped to his feet, staring out at the yard. Then, he leaped off the porch and into the grass. Emily followed his gaze, and saw a golden shimmer near the rose bushes. She whistled sharply—to her delight, Aunt Martha had taught her how to do one of those piercing "stop everything!" whistles with her pinkies—and Zack instantly turned to look back at her.

She pictured Marigold, and Zack responded by barking at the gold shimmer. As Emily watched, the shimmer turned into golden mist, and slowly took form. Then, Marigold was standing there in the sunshine, wagging her tail.

Emily turned to grin at Mrs. Griswold. "Look! There she is!"

"I don't see anything," Mrs. Griswold said testily.

Oh. Emily whistled again, and motioned with her arm.

"Can you please stop making that infernal noise?" Mrs. Griswold asked.

Both dogs bounded up onto the porch.

Okay, Zack was the key. What was the word? She totally had it in her vocabulary—somewhere.

Conduit! That was it. He was the connection.

"Put your hand on Zack's back for a minute," Emily said.

Mrs. Griswold sniffed. "I'll do no such thing."

It was hard not to sigh. "Please?" Emily asked.

Mrs. Griswold rolled her eyes, but touched Zachary's back.

Emily could sense that Zack was concentrating as hard as he could, so she did, too.

And it must have worked, because suddenly, Mrs. Griswold gasped and yanked her hand away.

"That's—I can see Marigold," she said, stuttering. "I—she—I can't believe it."

Marigold wagged her tail, and put her front paws up on Mrs. Griswold's lap, and to Emily's shock, Mrs. Griswold hugged her dog and began to cry.

"Will she stay here?" Mrs. Griswold asked Emily, still crying.

Marigold was already getting a little shimmery again, so Emily knew the answer. But, she didn't have the heart to say so.

Marigold let Mrs. Griswold hug her for another moment, licked her face, and then sailed gracefully off the porch. She almost seemed to skim across the grass, and then she stopped out on the dirt road, looking up at something.

Emily saw the familiar mist, and then, Mr. Griswold was there, looking more shimmery than she had ever seen him.

Mrs. Griswold gasped. "Sam!"

Mr. Griswold smiled such a loving smile at his wife that Emily felt tears in her own eyes. He put his hand to his heart, and held it there. Then, he made a hugging motion with his arms, while Marigold wagged her tail joyfully back and forth.

"Sam," Mrs. Griswold said softly. "Oh, *Sam*."

He lifted one hand to his ear and held it there, making a motion with his other hand as though he might be using a telephone.

"I don't understand," Mrs. Griswold said through her tears.

Mr. Griswold did another pantomime of making a telephone call, and then pointed at her. Then, he reached down to pat Marigold, and Emily could see the same golden shimmer start to surround him, too. He winked, raised his hand as though he was saying good-bye—and then, they both disappeared in a small flash of bright gold light.

Mrs. Griswold kept weeping, and Emily stayed right where she was, not sure what to do, or say. Zack had trotted back up onto the porch, and Emily patted him, trying to think of a graceful way to leave.

Mrs. Griswold was the kind of person who had an old copper cowbell hanging on a rope by the front door, instead of a normal doorbell—and when it rang loudly, Emily ducked.

"It's okay," Mrs. Griswold said, smiling through her tears. "He's just making a joke." She laughed weakly. "He loved movies."

Emily didn't *get* the joke, but that was okay.

"He looks wonderful," Mrs. Griswold said, with true wonder in her voice. "He looks *radiant*."

That was a perfect description, so Emily nodded.

"I don't understand any of this, but—" Mrs. Griswold shook her head as though she was trying to clear out some cobwebs. "You and the Percival boy are building a boat, correct?"

Emily nodded.

"You'll need something special for the prow," Mrs. Griswold said, and then reached over to pat Zack affectionately. "A dog, maybe?"

Definitely! "That would be—wow," Emily said. "Thank you. I would love that."

"I'll need you to bring me a block of wood," Mrs. Griswold said briskly, "when you can. I'm going to be laid up for quite some time, and—I like to keep my hands busy."

Emily nodded eagerly. How neat would it be to have a gargoyle of *Zack*?

"Well," Mrs. Griswold said, and picked up a portable telephone, which was on the end table. "I appreciate all of this more than you will ever know, but I need to be alone now. I have a long overdue phone call to make."

Emily nodded, and got up from her chair. Zack followed her cheerfully down the steps.

"Hello, Hank?" she heard Mrs. Griswold saying into the telephone, as they walked towards the front gate. "This is your mother."

Emily grinned. Unless she was completely off-base, that sounded as though the task had been completed!

Zack was feeling very bouncy, so she let him jump over the gate before she opened it. She was feeling pretty bouncy herself, and if she weren't twelve, and *beyond* cool, she maybe would have skipped.

They were about halfway home when Zack stopped. He was looking up at the sky, and Emily saw something drifting down towards them. They both watched curiously as the object floated very, very slowly in their direction. Finally, it wafted all the way down to the ground and landed right in front of them on the ground.

It was a feather.

A *beautiful* feather.

The colors didn't look quite real—sunshiny yellow with flecks of scarlet and blue, and a bright white quill. Emily picked it up carefully, not wanting to damage it in any way.

She held the feather out to Zack, who sniffed it delicately, then barked.

"I think it's a present," she said.

Zack barked again, so enthusiastically that she decided that her guess must be right.

She let the feather rest on her palm, noticing how warm it felt. It really was one of the most beautiful things she had ever seen.

When they walked into their backyard, her parents were sitting out on the deck, drinking iced tea and reading. Her father saw them first, and lowered his book.

"Mama!" he said, with what might have been an attempt at a Southern accent. "Look who's come back from the war!"

Emily and her mother both laughed.

"We were beginning to think that we might have to come down and rescue you," he said.

"What did she want?" her mother asked curiously.

Emily sat down at the table, while Zack went over to his water dish and drank heavily—and noisily—for a long time.

"I think she wants to be a better neighbor," Emily said.

Her parents waited expectantly.

"And—she likes Zack," Emily said. "Since she used to have a dog. When's supper?"

"About fifteen minutes," her mother said. "I just want the macaroni and cheese to crisp up nicely."

Cool. She liked macaroni and cheese. And Zack *loved* it.

Her father noticed the feather, and leaned over to look at it more closely. "Well, that's awfully pretty. Where did you find it?"

Emily pointed out at the road. "On our way home."

Her father squinted at it, through his glasses. "I don't think I've ever seen plumage like that before. What on earth kind of bird could it have been?"

Not on earth, was Emily's guess.

"Maybe we should take it over to the biology department, and see if they can identify it," he said.

Emily shook her head. "No, thanks. I don't really *want* to know." Which was totally and completely true.

"I just maybe want to hang it over my desk, and be able to look at it."

"Well, it's certainly spectacular," her mother said. "We can get a little frame, to protect it, if you want."

Emily nodded. "That would be great, thanks."

They ate dinner out on the deck as the sun went down, and the moon slowly rose over the quiet sea. None of them really spoke, because it was nice just to be together, and outside, and enjoying the evening.

"Oh, look!" Her father pointed up. "A shooting star!"

Emily glanced up just in time to see it streak across the night, followed by a second one. "Hey, there's another!"

"Right between Orion and Sirius," her mother said.

Emily knew that Orion was a constellation of a man, who was maybe an archer or a hunter. "What's Sirius?" she asked.

"The Dog Star," her mother said. "According to the myth, he was Orion's dog. It's supposed to be the brightest star in the sky."

A man, and his dog.

Well, of course. What *else* could it be?

Zack barked happily, and Emily bent down to give him a huge hug.

"It's perfect, isn't it, boy?" she said.

She could have sworn that he actually nodded at her, and then he leaned against her, looking up with adoring brown eyes. Brown eyes, with maybe *a little* speck of gold.

They all watched as the two shooting stars journeyed across the sky, leaving behind two small bursts of golden light at the end of their path.

Emily smiled, feeling as though—even if it was just for a moment—everything in the entire world was *exactly* the way it should be.

That everything was absolutely perfect!